No destination

Juan Manuel Rodríguez Caamaño

No destination
Juan Manuel Rodríguez Caamaño

First edition December 2019
First published Mexico City, December 2019

"I could not dedicate this work to anyone but who has always accompanied me in my life, in any project, on any green or sinuous path, dedicated this novel to God because he has given me inspiration in each of nature's wonders."

INDEX.

No destination

Juan Manuel Rodríguez Caamaño

Chapter 1

- If you buy that one, I'll sign it for you right now. Apart from helping children with cancer.

He stared her in the eye pointing to the book that she was browsing at the time and which she had taken from the top of the pyramid of novelty books, that place where every writer wishes to one day be, the cusp of literature. Amy's gesture was awkward, she felt her space invaded, her first thought was that maybe that gentleman was the owner of that airport bookstore and wanted to give her a book, an adult stranger trying to woo her, or just a dareful tourist looking for an adventure, which she found unpleasant. So, he didn't even have a look for him, he ignored it outright.

That Friday, September 28 minutes before six o'clock in the morning, even though the end of summer was recent, it felt a mild cold in Mexico City. The crystals looked foggy with a few drops sublimating to each span. Through them the sky looked dark blue, that tone that almost is confused with black, unlike the first very light flashes of clarity that began to permeate and barely notice each other in a less dark tone.

- What's more, I have an excellent offer that you will not be able to refuse.

She continued to ignore him, but now discovering a bare of annoyance at his comments. It used to happen to her frequently that some individual approached her with the intention of seducing her, it was not for less, every part of her looked perfect; her abundant eyebrows inherited from her father adorned her majestically her gaze captivating anyone from the first moment they saw her, were honey color but of an unusual, unique clarity, her hair was of a natural light chestnut, her lips were so beautiful that anyone who saw her **the first thing that came to mind was to bite** them, especially when she wore a crimson lip color, it seemed an unimaginable combination. But the brightest thing about her was her intelligence that stood out from the first word of any conversation, she always had the exact word for every moment, to make you laugh, ecstatic, comfort and even to hurt.

Faced with Amy's distrust, he pulled a book out of his backpack and showed it to her, noticing her forced gaze refusing to flip, **put it right in front of** her eyes, which annoyed her even more, and when she was about to insult him for his daring she realized that it was the second part of the book that was on display on the shelf, which just fade a little.

- Do you work for the bookstore? Or do you get commission for every book sold? - expressed with a derogatory tone still irritated but no longer by thinking of a courtship on his part but now imagining that he was some annoying seller stalking her until he achieved his goal.

Maybe Juan Manuel's guy fit more into the seller's profile than the stalker, a womanizer or writer. Already passing the spring of life approaching the middle of the century, his hair was scarce and mostly white. His beard had different shades such as a rainbow, white, black, brown and reddish. He never imagined reaching out in his fifties, but most likely he did. His body was already sturdy of an average lord, he was never physically attractive, nor in his youth, his only virtue was to write which is what he was most passionate about in life. In this way he had been able to captivate the few women who had existed in his life who had the fingers of one hand.

- No, miss, but I highly recommend that book, it is a *Best Seller* in all Spanish-speaking countries. If you acquire it, I'll give you the second part that's this. - pointed his index finger back at the cover of the book he was carrying. - Just published, you can't deny me that it's a great offer.

- Look no offense sir, - Amy said with a rather **irritated** tone, - but I haven't asked for any recommendation, plus I don't know if it's the kind of book I'm looking for, it seems more like a story for people your age. -   Sor sarcasm was obvious and instead of disturbing Juan Manuel made him suck slightly by stopping that happiness in front of her face still annoyed.

- I think you will like it. Tell me, who hasn't fallen in love with someone at some time **in** their life?

"I'm not that kind of woman looking for an adventure in a bookstore, or the kind that likes such extreme romantic stories - she said it as she read the book's synopsis, with that comment she expected to make you give up your sexual intentions if he had it. Her age made her distrustful of the intentions of any man who approached her, and that tender, irritated look denoted mistrust.

- There is only one way to know, I just want you to buy it to help a good cause, it is not my intention to even woo you, I am much older than you. Don't you realize my years? - with that statement he hoped would end at once with the presumption that he wished to seduce her.

- Ok, I appreciate your interest. I'll see other options before and after I decide.

She turned around, tried to rush out of the store to get rid of that alleged stalker, courter, salesman and deranged gentleman. But he stood in front of her again, breaking his escape.

- I think it's perfect only that at any time I'm going to tackle miss, so don't take it the wrong way, but if you decide you'll only get the benefit of helping the foundation of children with cancer, but I will no longer be able to give you the second part of that story and sign both tomes.

She let out a slight mocking laugh, already desperate to evade him.

- And why would you have to sign me or give me a book? Do you have a writer's complex? Do you feel Octavio Paz or Juan Rulfo in your spare time? Or are you the owner of the bookstore or the publisher and will you authorize me a gift copy to look good with me and show me how important it is?

He pulled out of the inside bag of his grey blue checkered bag, his ticket to board the plane and put it just below the bottom of the book where the author's name was located, which matched letter by letter with the name printed on the ticket to board Flight 627 to Cincinnati.

Chapter 2

She let out a laugh defending her attempt at runaway and blushed.

- Are you serious? I can't believe it, I'm sorry Juan Manuel, I thought you were bumping me off just to talk to me, so I didn't pay attention to you.

- First, she ignores me and now she tweets me - he let out a joke with her. - I know, that's why I insisted, how do you think I'm going to want to flirt with you, how old are you?

- I have just turned twenty-seven, and you Mr. writer?

- Forty-two, I will be forty-three next year, I am fifteen years older, a lifetime. I don't know how you think I want to harass you.

- With men you never know, the same and like to be Sugar Daddy – she said laughing. - Ok, you've convinced me, more for how sorry I am with you, although I'm not sure I like to read the story, - let out a mocking laugh. - I will buy it and I want you to sign it to me, give me the second part of signed gift too, stop telling me about you at this very moment and if in the future there is a third of the novel I want your serious commitment to send it to me to read before anyone else.

- It's a good thing about your deal, but I accept it in order to win one more reader in my audience.

- Perfect, don't say anything else, deal done. –

She trained in line to pay for the store book and some other baubles to eat during the flight.

- Would you like something to drink? Let me invite you something to correspond to the unexpected gift you're going to give me, - he immediately took a beer from the fridge and handed it to her.

- Beer? So early?

- I need to relax, I go to a presentation of the book you just bought and I'm a little nervous, it's my first time.

- You're old enough for your first time, aren't you? - let out another malicious laugh and sneer at the sexual connotation she had given to her commentary. He also responded by laughing at her unexpected comment.

- You trolled me, you have a dirty mind, and apart you do not respect my gray hairs, - they both let go another laugh - after all that initial tension between them there was already a great camaraderie.

- I'm sorry, my mother is veracruzana and in Veracruz are very foul-mouthed and worse thought out, but I was born in Sinaloa, like my father, in Guasave, do you know there?

- The most beautiful land in the world, Veracruz, I am from Coatzacoalcos the place where the snake is hiding. I don't like knowing your land, but just hearing the word Sinaloa makes my mouth water to think of the rich shrimp tacos with cheese that they sell in various places across the country called "governor" from over there. - Sinaloenses are very famous for that and good for other things not as nice as exotic agriculture, let's call it so, which is practiced in that area - she fused a rogue smile knew that her land was famous for the illegal plantings of various banned substances. Now I know why Maradona chose to lead the Dorados of Sinaloa, - laughed sarcastically - he knew that there he would feel at home.

- Hey, don't mess with the Dorados, for sure the Veracruz Red Sharks are very good. - apparently, she also liked football as I did. - Well when you go to Sinaloa let me know and I will take you to the best places I promise you, you will try the richest governor tacos of your life. - She raised her hand solemnly sealing that promise. – But I do not commit to the other thing that makes us famous I do not consume that kind of thing, but if you do it you are free to try wherever you want.

She joked again as she began drinking beer sitting on the benches of the waiting room while autographing the two books.

- It's a fact that I will go, apart I don't know if I know if to tell you that you have a somewhat complicated character, but all I have heard from Guasave is that they have an international dispute against galicians to determine who owns the copyright of all the countless jokes made with them. - She smiled in a beautiful way.

- Damn, I knew you wouldn't stand the urge to make fun of my land.

- I'm sorry, but it assumes that Guasave's are the Mexican Galicians, that's almost internationally famous.

- I will get even when I know your land, this will not stay that way.

- Don't be vindictive, then, is it true everything that is said in your jokes?

- And I hope that doesn't, - she said laughing - but well many Galician jokes make them, but with guasavenses.

At that moment he imagined her traveling by his side to a very beautiful place; The one he chose in the free will of his mind to know, his first thought was Cincinnati **because** it **was his** next destination, which he could not reveal to her because she would think he was trying to woo her, apart from that it had not crossed his mind until that moment when he saw her radiant smile. He took the pen and began to write her name on the lapel and a personalized dedication, just for that tender, innocent smile that had brightened the expectation of the journey.

- To?

- Amy, don't give me the classic dedication for all the customers "with love" for Amy and that's it.

- Apart from the squeamish, demanding, they are not my clients are my readers and I always sign something personalized, to see you what you are most passionate about?

- Read, I love reading all kinds of genres, if I told you a long time ago that I was not interested in the genre of your book was because I thought your intention was to approach me and not sell your book. –

Her taunts already became constant and I liked them, that meant she had confidence. With that information I was able to sketch out a few lines in a few minutes and then hand over the two copies.

- Ready, they are already dedicated. - She tried to open it **and read the** dedication, but he stopped her soft hands with hiss. - So, I'm going to ask you, to read the dedication when you're flying to your destination, please, it's my only request.

- Why so much mystery Mr. Writer? - She said with a sarcastic tone as she stared at him - don't believe it! don't worry about it, I'll watch the dedication at the end and take advantage to read them ,at the end of the day, it's a flight of almost four hours.

- I thank you, that you have then an excellent trip, enjoy the places you visit, it was a pleasure to meet you Amy...

- Collins, Amy Collins, my grandfather was Irish.

- All right Amy Collins, enjoy your flight and reading, I'll drink an Irish beer in Cincinnati to your health.

- Thank you I will do the same by reading Psychoaffaire and with a coffee.

We said goodbye with a kiss on the cheek, a tender brotherly embrace and a big smile, hers was masterful, unique.

She was flying to Houston just at the same time, but by gate 27, I watched her take every quick step, until she was slowly getting lost among the other passengers, lights and nearby shops; I tried until the end of following her with my gaze, but that red blouse point was getting smaller and when I tried to make my body right so as not to lose her, I bumped into that kid who played on the floor, she disappeared.

After an hour waiting for my flight announced, sitting at the door where I would board, I would write some ideas on my phone of what I had come up with would be my next novel. I found it unusual so many people concentrated in the waiting room in a not-so-demand time, so I approached the counter to ask what was going on because on the monitors showing the strangely several flights were delayed.

I hadn't observed that coincidentally they were all the first to leave, those at six a.m.

The hangover from a night out in Mexico City had left me a little dazed, but I realized this until the lady who attended the information desk told me the airport was closed because of the fog in the city , no flight had been able to take off, they were all delayed. How I didn't figure it out before if the airport became increasingly crowded and no departure or boarding was at least announced, only the numbers of the lounges in which each passenger should wait.

Flights leaving an hour before mine had not even boarded for this phenomenon, which very optimistically gave me at least two hours to get bored more waiting with a terrible headache or try to do what I do when I have to wait : write some history.

But at the time it was the least I wanted, I had a deadly debate between my hangover headache and an immense urge to sleep because I only rested for a couple of hours. I hadn't complained about the little rest, I'd had a nice night dining with my ex-girlfriend.

With the dehydration I had not the most bolder could write, I had no head for it, the more minutes spent the more people the area was filled, to the end of not being empty seats and many passengers faced with the accumulation of people for delays chose to sit or lie down in the aisles.

I was years old when I didn't hear that almost instrumental song, - "Whispering Wind" by Moby,- which reminds me of when I fell in love as a teenager already at an age fair to the woman I dined with a few hours earlier, it sounded in that bar called "Room 21" I imagine being located next to gate 21 to board.

I've always believed in fate, so for me those notes were a sign to get into "Room 21,"apart from what I imagined from the high prices of this and, was the only part of the airport where there were still empty places, all the other restaurants and chairs in the room were full. So, I decided to go in, sit down and order an espresso to wake up, a large bottle of water so I wouldn't get dehydrated, and a little tomato juice with lemon and clam to combat a little the hangover.

- Can I sit down? - I couldn't believe it, even a few drops of coffee spilled over by nerves, she was standing in front of me, with that gesture that moments before she was hard and now denoted confidence with a beautiful smile, requesting to sit at my table.

Chapter 3

- Why not, sit beautiful reader.

Everything was full, obviously also had her delayed flight which was to some extent understandable her appearance there at my table, so I turned to see around and there were still empty places in that restaurant, so at least form all the boring places at that time she chose to be in front of me and sat down.

She had the first volume of "Psychoaffaire: of Love and Death His Brief Passage" in her hands and the separator indicated that she had already read a third, in just twenty minutes, time that had passed since our farewell. I was flattered. We chatted the two hours of waiting and knew each other as their taste for reading and art; her fears of cockroaches and dread of flying women, her favorite places, her few short romances; even the most rugged politics where fortunately we were both anti-populists, Catholics and very fanatical to football, fortunately by the Veracruz blood of their mother was also fan, although not as a first choice of red sharks. Until we got to the most trivial issues and where we should logically have started.

- What will you do in Houston?

- I will visit a friend who has just gone to college in Austin and asked me to accompany her for a week so she wouldn't feel so alone. Since we were little girls, we've always been friends sharing important moments like we're sisters, so I take the opportunity to see her because she'll spend a lot of time there. - What will you do in Cincinnati apart from the presentation of your book?

- I also go to a conference of writers that there are on these dates and I take advantage to get to know the city, they say that it is very nice and in photos I have observed several very nice places.

- How interesting, one day I will be in one of your presentations and I will remind you of the awkward way how we met.

- I would love you to join me in some, although I think I would get a little nervous after our strange way of getting to know us.

- Since you publish your next novel, make a presentation in Guasave and I promise to organize every detail, we do not have such nice places for cultural events, but I guarantee you will love what I will plan with great affection for you.

- I like the idea of meeting over there, do you know Cincinnati?

- No. - she made such a nice gesture in her look and her lips when answering, that gave me a lot of tenderness. - I hope one day to be able to go to that place, I have been told that it is like a giant work of art, its parks and public square.

- Yes, that I have seen in photos and read in the comments on the internet, that is why I like the idea of going and being able to take advantage of those beautiful landscapes to have the inspiration to write in my spare time, that kind of cities makes my creativity flow naturally and more in a temperate climate as it is supposed to start autumn. Drinking an espresso and feeling the icy wind on my cheeks is an indescribably fascinating feeling for my mind.

The first flights of the morning began to announce their boarding which gave me at least three more hours to talk to her. Her flight was also leaving at nine, so we ordered some breakfast.

- What is your ideal breakfast?

- Fluffy waffles with lots of butter and just a touch of maple honey, accompanied by a natural orange juice and a pretty sweet espresso. You've already made me feel like it.

-Ok let me see what I can do for you, although I doubt, they have natural juice here.

I called the waiter and fortunately they had everything she had described minutes before, so I ordered that as is to make her feel at ease. For me I just ordered some toast.

- What's your ideal breakfast? don't tell me what toast.

- Believe it or not to be my favorite, toast smeared with butter and jam, accompanied by a rather sweet espresso just like you.

When I gave the first sip to that delicious espresso my ideal breakfast seemed even better with its smile in front of me. However, I tried to disguise that I liked her smile too much to avoid going back to that beginning when she imagined me trying to seduce her. And the truth was that hadn't happened in my mind until I saw her drink that espresso delicately with her lips. My mind only imagined them all over my body, I felt a little ashamed to wish so much at that moment such a young woman. But, above all, I was concerned that she might notice that I liked so many things in her and could be upset again, so I tried to be very subtle in every gesture.

- Your favorite food?

- Chinameca meat with sausage and beans.

-I don't know what that is, but I imagine it must be something typical of where you live, so I think if it takes until mealtime it will be impossible for me to fulfill your ideal meal as you have done with my breakfast.

- No need beautiful and I hope we are not until mealtime here either.

- Why? Have you been bored with my talk?

- Of course not. - She made me laugh too much with her occurrences, I think I liked that more than her physique which was also too attractive. - I urge you to arrive in Cincinnati to prepare everything for my event, we have already wasted a lot of time here, imagine if you give us the time of the meal here means that we will arrive at night to our respective destinations.

- That's why I'm lost time. - definitely her insistence began to reveal something of interest in me, or maybe I was misinterpreting it.

- On the contrary, if it were not for you I would have missed the time so quickly, it is more tempted to tell you that you were now part of my ideal breakfast, but I feared that you would still feel harassed so I better keep my comment, Ups! **I said it or I thought** about it?

She was laughing at my comment, so much so that she spilled her coffee on my pants, pretended nothing was wrong, and I held the burning of coffee burning my leg for a few seconds.

- At least you'll remember me the whole trip when you see that coffee stain on your pants.

- Oh yes? Then I'll spill mine on your dress too, so you don't miss me either.

- It's no big time, remember that I will read your books, so I don't need any other souvenirs, don't be vindictive JuanMa. - Her answers were always so clever that it was impossible not to let her own beat her.

- You win, but if we get to the meal let me buy you a glass of wine to find out what your favorite wine is, by the way, you haven't told me what your favorite food is.

- I didn't tell you because you haven't asked me, - her mocking smile was already frequent in our conversation - but my favorite dish is lasagna, that's why I made water in my mouth when you mentioned the wine glass because it's usually accompanied by a red wine, I love wine as long as it's red and it's not Cabernet Sauvignon because it's too acidic for me.

- Waffles? Lasagna? Don't women take too much care of their diet?

- Do you think all women want to be models or TV stars? No Mr. Writer, we have women who can live off things unrelated to our body, the body ends with time.

What a pleasant time I was going through with her, so pleasant that time flew by and those three hours had become a few twenty minutes in my mind and I felt the hands of the clock become a wagon carried to the precipice without stopping , which was his departure.

- You're also sure to be an environmentalist.

- Logic would call it me, if we do not take care of our environment, where will we live in the future? People like you live in the present without worrying about how we will live tomorrow.

- Hey! Who told you I'm not an environmentalist? I believe that the reason for the proliferation of all diseases in the world, such as cancer, is because everything on the planet is already contaminated, nothing is saved, neither the air, nor the land, that is why everything we eat is contaminated and causes so much degradation health.

- I agree with you, although you have no face to be an environmental defender.

- I don't need to be a radical to defend the planet and tie myself to a shrimp boat.

- Are you telling me I'm radical?

- Yes, but not for that, - now I returned her sarcasm - do not believe, - we laughed more and more, and her smile was being recorded in my mind as one of those pleasant memories difficult to remove from the memory. -   I feel shame of your boyfriend who has to endure your sarcasm; - to that assertion was not in order to joke with her, but to know something that from the beginning intrigued me too, to know who was the lucky owner of that masterful smile.

- Well, he doesn't complain, he's not as weepy as others who are bigger. - She left her left eyebrow pointing at me with her gaze.

- It has its reward to endure any onslaught, however hard, in order to enjoy your indecipherable smile.

- Indecipherable? You're a writer. Who uses that word to define a smile? Although I don't know if it's a good or bad adjective, tell me what it means in this context?

- Since I did not find an adjective that could combine all the beautiful qualities that I have observed in your smile in the short time of meeting us, I opted for one with a broader meaning, indecipherable means that you cannot understand if it is beautiful because you are happy, you probably aren't as much at the moment and yet radiates joy, if it's permanently cute because it's already part of you, or if it can be even prettier in pleasant circumstances.

- With pleasant circumstances do you mean that maybe I could be having a better time somewhere else?

- Why not? A couple of hours ago I was a stranger to you, so maybe instead of being with a man drinking coffee and chatting, you'd rather be in Houston with your friend, or in Guasave with your boyfriend, hugging.

- You went too far, but you stuck to the first two because in fact at this moment I am not in the most joyful stage of my life, my grandmother passed away a year ago and I still have too much pain in her memory and before I left I told my boyfriend that I needed some time so I could know what I wanted with him, however, my smile can't be prettier because I wouldn't want to be anywhere right now, in fact until I sat down and chatted with you in my mind was just thinking about not lengthening the delay of flights p I'm going to be with Mafer drinking a margarita and telling us everything that's happened in this time, but these last few hours I forgot everything else, thanks to you.

Her answer left me speechless, until now she had been very hard but now showing her feelings openly, so as I had nothing to say and not to look bad as a writer with a great imagination I decided to do operational things like order more coffee and ask her to trade our flights, that time served me to control a little the nerves that she had provoked me with her deep words that touched me to the deepest of my being.

- I had also thought of the infinite word to describe something so immense in beauty that the human mind could not understand in a simple way. - I was so afraid also to openly expose my thinking without disturbing her.

- No, indecipherable I like it more, no one had said me that word before and it sounds quite original, not trite, so don't compose it anymore that I don't know if I got scouted, but I loved your explanation, as a good writer.

- You have a very great faith in writers, sometimes writers only know how to write, and we are not good at anything else.

- Don't be modest, better tell me what your next novel is? - I nervously laughed at her question. She probably wouldn't like what I was writing.

- Do you really want me to tell you my idea?

- Yes, I promise not to tell anyone, I don't know any writer I can tell and steal your idea, so please let me have the scoop on what your new success will be.

- You don't want to hear it, I assure you.

- Why? Don't tell me it's something to do with bullfighting. I hate animal abuse, I don't know how there are people who can see that activity as a sport, even some as art.

- Worse than that, you better tell me about what you're going to do in Houston besides drinking margaritas.

- Don't tell me it's about rape, submission and outrageous things for women? Tell me and then I'll tell you about my plans in Houston.

- Much worse than that, I'm sure you won't like listening to it so let's change the conversation.

- Don't run away cowardly! - it had already become customary for him to joke with me. - I give myself, which can be worse than that, anything related to war? Or some horror story?

- I do not run away, I only protect myself from your outrage if you find out what I am writing, a war would be nice to you after hearing the idea of my future *Best Seller*.

- You've already intrigued me too much, you can tell you're an excellent writer, you've already hooked me up with your mysterious story. Come on! Tell me, or do you have nothing on your mind and you're just bragging?

Chapter 4

Her comment made me laugh so hard that I could no longer contain, and I decided to tell her the script for my next novel. I sipped my espresso that wasn't so hot anymore, so I ordered another one from the waiter and took some air to watch her reaction.

- Ok, I expect you support what I'm going to tell you without start fighting. What's more, so you can verify that what I'm saying is real, do you see this open text file that I have on my mobile phone? - I showed her a few seconds the screen with a few lines written in a file so that she could read the first lines and be sure how the story unfolded. - I started a few minutes ago to write a novel that occurred to me the moment I saw you choosing books in the store. There you go, it's the story of a writer who's not me obviously because that didn't happen, but that it's me because that's what I imagined happened to me to create this narrative. He is waiting for his flight to Cincinnati, where he will present his new book and enters an airport book store, seeing his first novel written among all the works located on the cusp of the recommended novels, generates a nice emotion, indescribable in the writer's life. Then exactly what happened a few hours ago happens between us when we met, a girl with the tenderest smile he has ever seen, flips through his novel and he recommends it. She thinks she wanted to woo her incredulous doesn't pay attention, he insists making a double offer.

- Wait, that story becomes known to me, - he smiled mockingly again - you just made up that right now.

- Sure, I told you it's the most recent story I'm developing.

- No, I mean, right now you came up with the way of telling me that and it's not true that you were thinking of writing this story.

- I showed you my phone screen so you can read that story. - I pointed my index finger at the screen. - Here's even your name, veil.

- I'm sorry I didn't read anything you showed me, I pretended I was doing it, but I was thinking about something else at the time. – She was sorry, I showed her the screen again and now she did take a few moments to read the first lines, it was indeed that anecdote that was embodied there, and she was the protagonist even with her name, Amy Collins.

- Now you believe me? I already have until the end thought. - She nodded.

- Ah yes, what would be the end? They meet again at the airport months later, that's a very trite thing, isn't it? It reminds me of a super boring movie called "Before sunrise."

- No, that's not what follows, she has her flight to Houston and him to Cincinnati at the same time, this is where the part that you're not going to like comes in with how complicated you are. - I laughed now mocking her and instead of bothering she did too. - When she asks him, what is the most recent novel he is writing, he tells her that he will only tell you that secret while having a glass of wine at the winger's bar.

- Wine glass? Nine o'clock in the morning? Is that our story? Should I be a co-author, shouldn't I? But in this case, it would be better to have an espresso as we are doing right now. - She scared me and blew me up in laughter over so many questions that he threw me at the same time, but above all her great and charismatic way of saying them with those honey eyes besieged me.

- There are many questions, but we go in parts, in that history both flights are at night, that's why the glass of wine.

- I thought you'd already made me an alcoholic like you. - I was beginning to fall in love with her subtle way of hitting me all the time with her occurrences and making me laugh explosively, even when she made fun of me.

- It's not our beautiful story, obvious the story was born from how we met, but they change a lot of things, too many so you can't be a co-author, is my story, created by me, okay?

- Okay, keep me telling me what it ends up in, I want to know what's next after our espresso, Ah I know! I try to seduce you, or I'll kidnap you and I'll leave you in a tub full of ice while I call for you to look for you like that famous 1990s urban legend.

- I can't tell you the ending, but I'll give you a synopsis of what happens in the development of the novel.

- Ok, tell me, maybe your story turns out to be a prophecy and everything goes on as it is, as a mystery film.

- I don't think that's what you want after you hear it, but well it goes on when she...- When I went telling her my whole story her face paled and I didn't know if it was of concern, admiration or nerves. – Then, with the taste of wine on her lips, he begins to tell her the story of his novel as I am doing with you right now, explains that she is the protagonist while she reads the dedication, which is in fact very similar to the one I put in your book; she is surprised and when she tells her that in the story the girl being reflected in the protagonist of the novel and with those beautiful words that she dedicates to her, she decides to change her flight to evoke the end of the idea she has for her story. She changes her ticket to Cincinnati, they travel together and the end I can't tell you or imagine one and you mail it to me the same and I choose that one, and maybe I can include you as a co-author. - I started laughing non-stop and she had no choice but to do the same until with the confidence we already had she confessed to me what I was thinking.

- What a good story, Mr. Writer, and this is where I run to change my flight to go with you?

- First I do not know if you can change a ticket that way, it is fiction; in second is just a story that occurred to me like many more who are born when I'm relaxed and stress-free, calm down I know it's crazy, that's how my stories are normally, but that's why it's fiction and that's why I like to write, because there I can do anything , create a world or disappear it, think of stories that might never happen to me in real life, and in third you were the one who came here to sit at my table and at that moment my story was already thought out, best of all, that talking to you has given me a good idea of how it can be such a relationship with the age difference, the things they would talk about, what each character would think. I don't really have contact with many people your age.

- Now I'm to blame?

- I didn't mean that, it was just an argument for you to see that I'm not making anything up. - Again, she was making fun of me and far from bothering me, I loved it.

- I cheated on you.

- What do you say? - I looked at her strangely, had no idea what she was talking about.

- I started reading your story and I liked it so much that I did not contain the desire to read the dedication.

Rarely have I felt as sorry in my life as in that instant, I thought that I would never cross word with her again so I had put those words a little up in in her copy, now I had to face my words and what she might think.

- Thank you very much for being the inspiration of this story that will be shaped forever and for being part of something important in your life, becoming immortal as you say in your dedication, but above all for imagining that I am with you in the most important moments. No one had ever made me feel so transcendental in my life and I'm not kidding. - His countenance of happiness became a serious one when he mentioned these words, he did not know what to say so we just stood by each one looking at each other on both sides of the table so as not to cross glances and force us to disguise, I felt like a teenager feeling that nerve how strong you talk to the person you like for the first time.

She asked for the account of the place and paid for it without me being able to do anything, I didn't like that, but she told me it was in compensation for the book I had given her and above all for making her the protagonist of my novel.

She rose from the table in a hurry without giving any explanation, I got up also trying to reach her.

- Where are you going?

- Follow me and you will see.

Chapter 5

I was going after her down the airport corridor following the rapid passage of her beautiful legs, trying to figure out what she would do. We walked to the halls at the beginning where there were some models of information and he arrived at the room where he would board his flight, took a deep breath and stared at me.

- I don't know how I finish your novel, **but I want to continue to be part** of her, I know it's probably the biggest madness you've ever heard and I've said but the truth so far no one had made me feel as important in this world as you, apart from my parents. I'll check right now if I can change my ticket to go with you to Cincinnati, and we keep writing this story there. Maybe in the middle of the flight we no longer support each other, **but at least it will help us to know** something different.

I was speechless, my story as I had imagined in my next novel was being fully fulfilled. I was tempted to stop her and tell her not to do that madness, but since I **first** saw her I imagined that look less than an inch from mine, well, intimidating me with the vast clarity of her pupils and feeling the moisture of her lips eager to keep kissing me. My God very young and me having those thoughts.

- Are you sure that's what you want?

She nodded and was not going to question her again, putting her intention at risk and regret traveling with me.

Life sometimes only gives an opportunity to be immensely happy and I thought about it so I headed to the counter with it, however, I knew how the airlines were operated and it was very complicated what we planned, chances are that our idea would die there **and it** was just an illusion of spending a weekend together, even more so because the time of boarding was coming. However, I could not help trying everything, like an evicted one seeing a small light of hope. I tried to be as optimistic as possible.

- Miss, good afternoon, look I know that what I'm going to ask you is very complex, but please could check if there is any possibility for Miss Amy traveling to Houston on the delayed flight of nine, I could change her flight to the destination traveling a server that is to Cincinnati at nine as well. It doesn't matter that I have to pay something extra for the change.

-Look, in theory we can't do that, besides it is likely that both flights come full. - her face said it all, she intended to support us, but it was not in her hands, the lady next door who seemed the one who was leading there I could hear.

- Are you Juan Manuel Rodríguez the writer of Psicoaffaire?

- Yes, at your service. How did you know?

- I really like you style, in fact, I'm reading this book now. - she showed me a copy of my novel "Always you" - I am fascinated by her stories because always love can clear any obstacle no matter if this is something impossible.

When that young lady made that comment, Amy gently lay her head on my shoulder very tenderly, at times I wanted to protect her as if she were a fragile child in my care, but at times all kinds of thoughts with her from the purest to the lowest passed through my mind.

I had to use all my tricks to convince the lady at the airline counter to change that ticket and I made it. Luckily I stumbled upon that avid reader and I knew who I was, I knew several of my works, I gave her several of the books I brought in my backpack and I autographed them almost for each of her loved ones who expressed to me liked to read, I committed to her to send her a copy of my next novel before it went on sale and I paid a small difference with my card the cost of changing the route, which was not allowed, but she politely, was willing to do whatever to enjoy that smile a few more hours, I finally made it. I was about to make the biggest madness of my life and I'm sure she did too.

- You haven't told me about yourself, are you married? Divorced? Separate? Free union? Committed? Sugar Daddy? Widower? Heterosexual? homosexual? Bisexual? - the intent of her question was more than obvious, to find out what my sentimental situation was before she takes any risks with me.

I made her think I was divorced so I wouldn't see her at a disadvantage with her having a relationship and maybe I was just a man excited about her and the next day I wouldn't even turn around to see. Besides, I was a little embarrassed that she at her age had a boyfriend and I, at the age of 43, had no one, single and childless, which is not an excellent cover letter for an older man like me.

- She must have been very lucky to have someone so talented by her side.

I quickly changed the subject so as not to give details that could show the veracity of what I was saying. How could I talk to her about my love life if it was something rather boring as well as my life?

The only thing I knew how to do was write, other than my failures in life were countless, as an athlete I tried to play football, but I never had the necessary physical condition and the courage to achieve it. At school I was the chubby, high-score child, "nerd" as they are called in many places, being bullied and sought after even at university by beautiful women just to do some homework or help them study as that friend used in emergencies for some exam.

It is difficult to summarize the story of my life that I was not proud of, from which I often wanted to flee, that I was ashamed to remember, because sometimes childhood and memories of youth are not always beautiful as everyone thinks, there are memories that are worth forgetting.

Chapter 6

I fell in love so many times in life, however, it was all **great disappointments, most of the time it was of** women who didn't feel the same way about me. As a child I remember Alicia, my primary school classmate, with whom I couldn't even cross the word. It was such my shyness that I was terrified of approaching her, which became worst in high school when I saw how that intelligent girl named Karime was a distant dream because **being more and more friends confessed to her became something** even more complicated, an impossible task, like scorning that beautiful friendship for an attraction. In college it was the same, I fell platonically in love with my two best friends Ana and Claudia, who never saw me with eyes that were not friends.

I remember the first time I really fell in love, I gave everything, my time, my effort to pamper her at every moment and she was just thinking of being with that married man who almost doubled her age, when I offered her my whole life; I remember when she broke up with me I begged her like I never preached begging anyone. She was my student in that class that most observed boring about literature, it was the first time I gave classes a few months after I graduated from university, however, she was the most outstanding and interested in the subject, we developed a great friendship that at the end of this became something else, the relationship became closer in every second that we saw each other until I almost got lost in her gaze. She was the first woman to ever kiss and it was an unforgettable thing.

When I **found out she was dating** with me, **but also with** that guy, I got **an angry rage that** I couldn't close my eyes all night for all that negative energy running through my body, it was the adrenaline overflowing to do something, I thought of even the worst things, my angry mind came to kidnap her, hurt her, I had never felt so much love and love at once.

At times I wanted to generate a lot of pain and in others I wanted him to just repent and come back to me, which is difficult to fall in love for the first time, but above all that it is hard to do in lost as it is of someone who does not feel the same thing.

A friend of hers told me where to find her, leaving that fancy hotel in the city, I waited for her and when I saw her leave was so much my courage to see her with that guy that I took the wallet that I had given myself days before, I addressed them until I stood in front of her, threw the wallet on her chest and told her that I did not want to keep anything that she would have given me.

It was hard to forget her, I completely walked away from the lifestyle I was leading so as not to know about her, when someone tried to tell me something about her life changed the subject; until time did his thing and healed every wound.

The second time I fell in love was just as disastrous, I knew that she had a reputation for not taking the relationships seriously and knowing about it, I risked dating her but with the mentality that it would be nothing serious, I still do not know if it was the woman I fell in love the most because with her I made love for the first time; or if she was like a small doll, perfect, delicate, with each fine faction; or if I was a victim of her greater experience in love affairs. Whatever the reason, I only remember that night I said goodbye to her to travel to Cuba where I was doing graduate school. I even thought about deserting that dream of having a specialty for her. I traveled often but that time I felt something strange, I still remember how she cried, hinting that my departure hurt a lot, **even though** shortly after I left, she decided to finish. It took me years to hear that Polo Montañez song "A Lot of Stars" **without** draining a flow of tears. I even listen to her and my stomach gets churning, I remember like yesterday was her phone call asking me for time.

I did everything to finish the last exams early and run to the airport to change my flight; I didn't sleep to see her again, so I traveled and arrived two days earlier than predicted, dying **to tell her that I loved her.** The idea was to buy a bouquet with her favorite flowers, go to her apartment and enter with the key she had given me, leave the flowers in a vase and return the next day to talk to her and seek to reconcile.

It wasn't a good idea, I managed to get in quietly but when I got to her room I found her sleeping with someone else, a friend I had been in contact with when I was away; my heart was throbbing at a thousand an hour, wanting to get out of my chest, but before they saw me cry I left the room but inadvertently threw the vase I had given her on an anniversary with an orchid and they both woke up scared and in a heartbeat were standing in front of me. I just grabbed her shoulders tightly and told her I didn't deserve this, she asked me to leave her house and I did.

Outside it was raining and I could do nothing but stand in front of the entrance, with a great pain in the chest, letting the water soak me and thinking what I could have done so as not to lose it.

The third time was just as terrible; with the experiences I had had before, I had a hard time finding a woman I could trust, but I found her, compatible in everything, the same tastes and passions, even the same star sign. We were so confident, I loved living my day to day by her, traveling with her; it was the perfect relationship.

In addition to the large number of freckles adorning his cheeks I loved that particularity in one of them, a slight well that when making her smile appeared and I was fascinated to know that I was responsible.

Again, I did not know if it was my excess attention, my absolute dependence on her that bored me and changed me.

For no change, it was a rainy night in the city when I went to pick her up at that bar. I had been drinking and there was something in her hasty way of saying goodbye to me a few hours before, that it made me have a little feeling, it was a very big, dark place and I was a little, which made it a little difficult for me to find her, even after I had toured and I place several times. So, I decided to leave, for sure my drunkenness was such that I couldn't locate her.

I was about to cross the exit when under the stairs and in an even darker place I could distinguish her back hair, try to think anything but what was really going on, she was hugging and kissing a guy I had never seen and fortunately I've never seen again. I pulled her arm and I wanted to hit her for the effects of alcohol, but I held back, I couldn't miss that promise that one day I made my father of women never touch them even with the petal of a rose, So I contained all my fury and ran out of the place to cry to my car, with the sea of witness.

And so we came to the last time I fell in love and lost her for not deciding to be with her forever, maybe that was my greatest trauma in love, this time I was finally loved as I had so desired but the previous experiences left me so damaged with deception and forgetfulness that this time I didn't know how to keep the flame between us, a breakup that made me frustrated being my fault and at the same time by almost forcing me to think that that should be my life and being alone forever.

Perhaps it was the most painful defeat to lose her when I had everything to be happy with her, it was something that my immature mind did not appreciate or could not appreciate, summed up in a few words when I wore the loss loses and when I had everything to win also lost in love.

Until the day Amy appeared and let me see a slit of hope in believing that I could find my soul mate, the one who shared all my follies, considering that our friendship was given to the greatest madness that I remember in my life and I could almost swear q for her too, that madness was worth risking anything to try to fall in love again. However, she had a lifetime ahead of her and thousands of alternatives that could, in my view, meet all her expectations, my pessimism was not because I did not want to be with her, I wanted that from the moment I met her, my negativity was due to all experiences past and to that I felt that I was not good enough for her.

Still, bad experiences imprinted a fear for another possible love defeat and more for the age difference, which gave a little more uncertainty to this relationship, maybe I wasn't what she was looking for, but for me she was perfect.

Chapter 7

- Has it ever happened to you that they close the airport as today because of the fog?

- Yes, on one occasion traveling to South America.

- Then you should know how long flights are delayed.

- At least four or five hours; two or three hours of waiting for the fog to come down, one more hour of boarding and you have to wait like another hour already being inside the plane because if it takes all the flights depending on the sequence they are assigned by the large air traffic that usually is available, add the accumulated flights by the hour.

- Uff then we will get to dinner practically in Cincinnati.

Within a few minutes we were sitting in waiting room number 37 waiting for the time to start boarding, coffee always had the quality to increase my anxiety and at that time I was desperate to board, before she could repent.

I felt the icy skin just having it sitting next to me, I didn't imagine everything that could happen on that trip, not so much for the physical but for the emotional, doing crazy so it wasn't something that was done every day and it's just done by someone very special, maybe that made me more dreadful, thinking that this could make me feel things that I could not control, like imagining her smile all the time since we talked in the airport cafeteria and then it would go away and not know more about it , living with the pain of never seeing her again.

That worried me, but at the same time I liked to feel that shudder that ran all over my body. I felt like a teenager in his first love experiences. But what troubled me even more was her calmness, how I could be so relaxed when I was dying nervous about traveling with her. I was thinking about what to say every second, taking care of every detail. I went to the nearest café and had a tea to relax.

- How do we get your bag if you don't get to Cincinnati?

- What cares the suitcase, I buy the indispensable there, you do not worry, just concentrate on making an excellent presentation of your book so that I continue to feel proud of you as a writer. - She finished telling me that and turned again to the other side to settle down and continue reading the book I had signed for her from which only a few pages were left. We were short to board and we had to do it on our own because we were going in separate places approached me.

- How could you do that to Carolina? - she said turning to me again with that sarcastic smile, I just smiled and raised my shoulders trying to say speechless, sorry is just fiction. I put on a face of surprise and got up pretending to go to the bathroom, since I was a kid when I was too nervous I was urging myself to go to the bathroom, and this moment of leaving with that amazing woman I had met so strangely made my nerves on the tip.

When I came back, she was reading a social magazine with women's covers looking elegant and with spectacular bodies. I thought I was just killing her time, looking at her, but it was a few minutes past and I was completely focused reading.

- What do you read beautiful?

- An article on the incompatibility of signs

- Do you believe in those things? - I told him with a sarcastic tone.

- No, but because you are not otherwise aware of this nonsense, when is your birthday?

- Don't you think you're into that nonsense? - I said while I was dying.

- So, tell him your birthday **and stop being bitter** - I laughed for **the** gleeful ways he made the voice and scolded me subtly again.

- June 4th, what about you?

- On March 17.

- St. Patricks Day?

- It can't be! - put a face of feministic concern. - Virgo and Pisces are the least compatible signs with Gemini in love according to the article of this journal, scientifically demonstrated. - At first, they can get along well, but in the long run they will have trouble understanding each other-

- Really? Is that what you're saying? What fear to travel with you. - kept laughing when she winced quite a pimp. – If **you may have hope, you and I got off to a bad start at** the beginning, the same and it all gets better in Cincinnati.

Every movement on the hands of that Swiss wall clock in front of us became eternal, as if in slow motion I were anesthetizing every muscle of the body, which was shuddering and tingling through the nerves of the closeness of our departure.

There came a time when I no longer knew how to disguise it, my left leg crossed on the right kept moving intensely, my hands sweated a little which had never happened to me, I turned everywhere looking for a **topic to be able to talk with** it, even if it was the dumbest and most important, but every second that passed **my mind** was blocked more.

Just as we were about to board, she told me I should go to the bathroom, she ran fast until I lost sight of her. I came out of line to wait for her, even though those sudden urges to go to the bathroom made me too suspicious, I was terrified I felt the body cold to think she had repented and would never see her again. Moreover, several minutes had passed and he was not returning, all the passengers had already entered the plane and we were only missing.

She turned to see the clock and six minutes had passed and she didn't even show up down the aisle. The airline worker told me I should enter, I begged her to let me make an urgent call that would take me only a minute and although she did not accept I turned around and took my cell phone pretending that he made a call. He didn't even have his number to dial him, just his name and the constant memory of that smile.

   - Mr. Rodriguez, can't we wait for you anymore, will you board this flight or not?

Of course, I had to board it I had to fulfill my dream of making my book presented to American readers, I couldn't let them down, so I handed her my ticket to board and I entered the aircraft.

Chapter 8.

That crazy idea that went through my head took me too far by surprise. I didn't understand how my mind could come up with something as far-fetched as going with a stranger to Cincinnati, he had treated me with much cordiality and without any interest other than the one used when you have nothing to do and pay attention to the only person who is in your company, but the fact that his new novel was about me made me feel in the clouds. No one has ever given me so much importance.

I completely disconnected from the place and the company at that moment, by my mind passed, first of all, that maybe Juan Manuel could be a serial killer and that he wrote his works to women that he wanted to murder, I have always been very dramatic and extremist, also passed the age difference, surely was a womanizer who went around the world seducing young women by dedicating his works to them. My mind created thousands of theories per second to prevent me from doing something crazy; then I came up with a good idea at my head, maybe he had lied to me with his marital status and was a married man looking for an adventure because he was going through the crisis of 40 in which men look for young women to feel more virile and more men.

I pulled out my cell phone immediately without him noticing, I think he felt sorry because at that moment I was looking the other way, I settled it on my knees. My research skills should help to learn more about that charming writer. The first thing I found in his biography was his age, in which he had not lied, nor in his profession, I looked for his marital status and found several photos with a beautiful woman in which they mentioned was his girlfriend, but the dates of those photos were not recent , so I intuited that it was a past relationship. I found his Facebook page and there he said that his sentimental situation was single and then I smiled stupidly, I was glad to know that I was alone and then I realized that during the search my hands had been sweated from nerves, I didn't want to have a partner.

It was crazy just thinking about making his novel a reality and going with it, but in the back of my mind something said "do it", as if I were beginning to suffer a kind of chronic schizophrenia, that voice of my consciousness shouting "do it" became too much tea. If anyone knew everything that went through my mind, they'd think I was crazy and that I need to be admitted to a psychiatric hospital as soon as possible.

If I decided to board the flight, I wouldn't see my best friend too long and so it would be maybe a year or more, it hurt to think of not seeing her when she was one of the most important people in my life and the only one who fully understood me.

We were like Cristina and Meredith from Grey's Anatomy, my favorite series. Although I also knew that Mafer would understand my decision to change my destiny, after all, even if we saw a short time, she would always be my best friend.

I understood that I wanted to go to Cincinnati, that living that adventure would give a little excitement to my monotonous life, emotion that I had not felt in a while. To begin with I had never felt so trustful with someone as with Juan Manuel in such a short time, he had that quality of having achieved that effect in me, I never felt self-conscious with him to say what was born or to freely disturb him , sometimes my mood is heavy and his too, was an instant connection. Besides, on my wish list I was in the third place "do a crazy thing" and that adventure could well count as one. There was nothing to lose, at least nothing important. We could be friends, sleep in separate rooms and tour in their spare time, besides curiosity killed me for knowing more about the novel I was writing about me. Her intense Psychoaffaire novel made me feel sexually ill when I imagined him and me in some of those erotic scenes, but I felt so strange that I tried never to think again about those situations.

I made the decision, I wanted to keep the cell phone in my bag, but it started vibrating and I saw Ricardo's name on the screen.

I lost my smile; I had completely forgotten about him.

Ricardo was my boyfriend or maybe my ex-boyfriend, I had just asked him for time to clear up my ideas. As a man he was the dream of many, tall, with very good body, intelligent, extremely hard-working and, above all, he was crazy about me. Well because of the idea he had about the woman I could become if I wasn't so impulsive and unfiltered between my brain and my mouth.

At the beginning of our relationship I felt lost in love, only he existed in my world, until he felt confident enough to tell me that I did not always have to say my opinion and to ask me to take care of everything I posted on my social networks. I've always hated such restrictions, so at that point the infatuation started to fade away and I started to see him as a sexist man, that took me two years of my life. Still, I continued with the relationship, I do not know if out of love or by habit, sometimes he made me feel in the clouds and others he would drop me suddenly when I went out with some new criticism or when he started flirting, just like it was flirtatious and I had not noticed it until that moment and I allowed him to do it, in the end I never believed that he would be able to deceive me or leave me for someone else.

Thinking about Ricardo made me sad, I didn't know how, but if I were my everything, I had gone to be off my list of priorities. I loved him, that's why I was pretty sure, I just didn't know if I loved him as a friend or as a couple and that was the question of why I'd asked him for time to think. It wasn't easy after all these years together deciding to take him out of my life forever.

He was my first love, the first time I felt that someone needed me, the first time I felt desire for someone. He was the first man in my life and although the years passed, I always had something that no longer gets angry with him, I loved it. I had no other reference in terms of feeling something for some man, since I had only fallen in love once in my life, I had had many dates before Richard, but only with him I had a formal relationship full of love. Perhaps it was necessary and even healthy to be able to live other experiences to know if my feelings for Richard were still love, there was only one way to know and it was to live my life without fear of anything.

After that call that brought me back to reality, my reality, the decision had been made. I ran to the bathroom.

Chapter 9

I sat in the 17C seat with immense desire to cry with the frustration of having excited me like a little boy with that lovely girl, I had never been so fascinated by a woman in such a short space of time, that is why I illusorily believed that that relationship could grow to an exponential size, unthinkable every second. I got up from the seat as soon as the captain turned off the light of fastening the seat belts to go to the bathroom, although the nerves of traveling with her were diminishing her intensity, I now felt sad that she had not succeeded.

I opened the bathroom door and the water key, to slowly wet my cheeks and eyes with that elixir that my mother used as a child to wake me up and go to school, now that glare of moisture was confused with that of tears that she had denoted. I looked in the mirror and saw each of my features deteriorated over time and understood that maybe I wasn't important enough for someone like her, that She was a queen to someone as banal and uninteresting as me.

I returned to my seat moving a little from side to side, holding my hands on the headwaters of the seats before mine because of the slight turbulence that was shaking at my seat.

   - Sorry JuanMa had to do something very important before boarding, what do you prefer, hallway or window?

I was silent again to see that unique smile that I thought I'd never see again, I had asked my seatmate to change the place and there I was sitting with her beautiful cross legs covered by that white dress, in the seat next to mine.

Most of the flight time I used it to find a way for no one to notice her presence, devising plans and strategies, such as planning a perfect crime, before boarding she made a call to her friend with whom she would spend the holidays, which she would visit after me not to see her, to tell her how she should answer if someone in her family was calling for her since she had no signal on her phone during the flight. I had promised her that after the weekend she would travel to Houston to leave her personally at her friend's house and return to her normal life. I even saw her message her boyfriend before tackling as if she were making her original flight plan to Houston. Which, although I didn't like it at all, I decided not to pay attention, as I had barely appeared in his life.

I've never felt as nervous as those three hours of flying to Atlanta, followed for an extra hour to Cincinnati, I imagined that, if I enjoyed every moment locked in a plane with that girl, being with her knowing beautiful and unknown places would be a fascinating thing.

In the waiting room in Atlanta, every time I asked her if she wanted something to drink or eat to which she always answered with that angelic smile.

- I'm fine, don't worry about me, relax.

I've never met a woman so beautiful, unless I enjoyed and followed my follies. This time when boarding I felt very calm, compared to the stress I cause in the boarding of the first flight where I thought I regretted traveling with me and flying to its original destination.

Now as I lined up, I was not only by my side but also took my right hand with yours and so we stayed until we entered the cockpit.

Takeoff in Atlanta was fast unlike traffic at the already overrun airport in Mexico City. The best thing was that when the plane started to rise, she took my strong hand and was forced.

The first twenty minutes of the flight passed without further mishap, she fell asleep when she pushed back her seat and lay down, I tried to do the same until I was surprised just like her by that sudden blow at the head of my seat, but was not a blow, but the movement of turbulence that was beginning to feel inside the plane and that was quite strong, extending the time that we spent the time.

I was terrified, I had traveled countless times to many countries of the world, I knew almost every continent and had never felt movements as sudden as those that rocked that Boeing 727, I began to pray without her percussing so as not to alarm her and hoping that in the next second it would all return to normal, but suddenly my glass of wine leaped and stained her white skirt that covered her beautiful legs. On this occasion instead of causing me excitement I did not even pay attention to seeing her terrified face too, apparently, she had not had a turbulence of this magnitude either.

She told me with lips trembling with fear, because the turbulence that we had both experienced previously had been short and this time the plane seemed to fall into total control, everything was more shocking when the oxygen masks placed on the roof of the plane came out, stirred violently more and more, there came a time when our confidence that it would soon end that intense movement got lost. Minutes passed and everything moving louder and louder, many on the plane screamed in despair and the minute later they were mute to see that instead of giving in a little bit more and more.

Chapter 10

Finally we landed in Cincinnati at seven o'clock in the afternoon and the sky was completely dark, the wonderful lights of the city, seen from the air generated a feeling of nostalgia after the immense fear that we had passed when we felt the turbulence more atrocious than we had probably both lived.

We descended from the aircraft, still shaking from that dread that went through our veins from halfway to landing, shuddering. We picked up my bags and when we felt the fresh air of that warm Cincinnati night, she hugged me and started crying.

- I imagined my life together with my parents from when I was a child to their pain for anything that could have happened to me on the flight. - She said it referring to the extreme turbulence that we had experienced minutes **before, I embraced her, that moment was very traumatic for both.**

- I also felt the greatest fear of my life and saw it go my whole life, but above all those things that I would leave pending if something happened but thank God, we are alive, and we can enjoy one more day. - I pressed even harder until a few minutes passed and calmed down.

- You're right, so you must live to the fullest every day we spend together.

Your proposal was perfect. At the exit of the airport there was an information module. I took several brochures that were around with tourist attractions of the city to have nice places to meet next to it.

- Watch these brochures to review what you would like to do in your stay here.

She turned to see me with a tender face of lust that I felt totally intimidated. She snatched from my hands all the leaflets I had collected and before crossing the exit door she threw them in the first recycled trash can I saw or in his wake and began to laugh with laughter, which surprised me by how intimidating, but at the same time I liked it.

- Fulfill what you promised me in your dedication, we don't come for a walk, you understand me? - He closed his claim with his classic cheeky smile while I headed to get a taxi to go to the hotel.

What I was thinking when I put those words, if only she knew I was writer because it is easier for me to express myself and give my opinion on certain topics.

Heading to the hotel in the taxi she nested between my shoulder and my arm and was completely asleep, we were both very tired for the trip, I could imagine that I more for my age, despite that, while I was asleep she drained a little saliva on my shirt and started to make some not-so-loud snoring and that I got a lot of tenderness.

We arrived at our destination and fought to wake her up, all I wanted was to get to sleep, there had been too many emotions for a single day. I managed to wake her up and bring her back to herself to ask for our room at the front desk. She was sticking to my shoulder I don't know if to lie down because she was tired, because she was affectionate with me or both.

- Are you tired? Do you want us to go and rest? - I asked her why I saw her squint.

- I finished reading the first tome of your book on the flight to Atlanta and the second part in what we expected the flight to Cincinnati and for the first twenty minutes before the turbulence. So, what you have to do is not think about where we'll know but where you're going to do all those romantic crazy things you wrote in those books. I do not know if there is a square of revolution here as in Havana; The most complicated thing shouldn't be that, but every public space here must be watched by camcorders, but we'll already figure out some madness like that from Psychoaffaire.

Her words shuddered me, although I knew beforehand that he did so for that reason, there was already great confidence between the two to be able to talk and joke about any subject however rough.

After the desperation we had just lived with the turbulence that made us think of catastrophic things, I think we both felt less stressed that we could live those days, reflect that our life could end at any time and living together that dreadful moment above the plane, had made us go from being two strangers to two people who could trust each other, every minute after that moment we saw it as a gift from God and an opportunity to enjoy its wonders and forget of so many prejudices.

It was already night and despite my tiredness we decided to walk around the hotel to get to know the places nearby. Everywhere we walked there was access, moving from one park to another and from one urban piece of art to another, it was a very well-planned city, ideal for walking and chatting with. To make it taken from his hand was a feeling he missed, to feel like the world for something as simple as having the person you like around is an indescribably beautiful feeling.

We toured those three stunning scenarios, almost side by side, was something unimaginable to me and even more so being able to access each one with great ease, and next to the most beautiful smile that had seen my eyes until that age. The majestic "Paul Brown" stadium of Bengali Football the most popular sport in North America, the diamond of Cincinnati's historic Reds baseball's "Great American Ball Park" sports king stage, and aside from the "US Bank Arena" formerly called " Riverfront Coliseum" venue concerts and the Cincinnati Cyclones city hockey team.

Cincinnati surprised me, it was the first city on my list where I could walk, climb and descend streets, sculptures and parks along the calm Ohio River. You could enter the afore mentioned stadiums or return to the city Centre very easily by pedestrian bridges, accesses, escalators and tunnels. It was a city with excellent planning, ideal to spend a perfect holiday with it, walking with the perfect woman who at that time was her.

We walked several minutes and crossed artwork, games for children, parks, stadiums, boats, bridges, I was impressed by their energy after such a heavy day and seeming to faint in the taxi. It seemed that I had recharged energy in the few minutes that slept soundly lying on my shoulder on the way from the airport to the hotel. I noticed that to get up the river to US Bank Arena there was a ladder that led both to the campus and the Stadium of the "Great American Ball Park" of the Cincinnati Reds and then went down an escalator that seemed always to be up and running even as we were approaching the night.

We moved on so much that we arrived very tired and fell in the hotel room without saying a word, the room number matched my lucky number on the 27th. The next day we got up very early, perhaps because of the difference in schedules and decided to go to tour again the places we walked the night before, although even the daylight did not arrive, everything was mist around, so we went back that way with a little more clarity.

I told him to go up that ladder that was still dark again, halfway through it you could see the first rays of the sun, but the fog blurred the road.

We wanted to see the sunrise and waited for it for several minutes and unlike many places in the world arrived almost at half a half in the morning those rays that illuminated the riverbank.

      - How cute the sunrise looks!

She didn't finish saying those words when, seeing her alone in front of me with that landscape, I started kissing her like I hadn't kissed anyone in my life, desperate to think I'd only be with her for a weekend.

I knew how dangerous it was to be there kissing, yet my mind became irrational and I turned it over abruptly, she didn't understand what was going on.

Chapter 11

Until she felt her back glued to my chest and I quickly lowered her trousers and mine, I was hoping at some point the probability of her resisting, but while I wasn't doing it I kept kissing her until I penetrated her, I could do it easily because I was at that moment more excited than ever, so that awkward position was not pretext. So we were while she said that someone could see us and tried unsuccessfully to get out of the way, but as much as I repeated it kept moving slowly enjoying the moment, I didn't say anything, I was perplexed, my legs were shaking because of my nerves and the position where I was holding her hip a little bit on me.

I had no idea what to say, I was so afraid to say something that would bother him, so I abstained from something tender or something dirty because I didn't know even what she liked sexually, in fact I didn't have time for it because I was totally focused on not finishing so fast because since I was inside it I was about to make it so excited that I was to **be with her for the** first time, the perfect moment with her, her smile, her body, the landscape of the first flashes of dawn over the river , were an indescribable landscape.

So I was with all my strength holding me about to explode for a couple of minutes until I felt her relax and her innermost part squeezed me even more in a sign that I was satisfied, that's when I felt like a flow of the river running in front of our eyes was running freely after being contained within it.

Every ray of sunshine over her pupils into that incredible, unrepeatable scene, I lifted my pants and hers that I could barely breathe, but we had to continue because it was already dawning. Just then an Asian runner walked by making a lot of noise.

We didn't say a word all the way back as we ran down the river and crossed the bridges we had passed earlier.

We were ecstatic and ran harder than ever before and at par, holding hands. I've never understood why women with adrenaline end faster, that was the kind of thoughts that stalked me as I held her hands.

- Did you mention this when you mentioned finding a place like the Revolution Square in Havana? - I said a little afraid that she might get upset.

- I meant to walk together holding hands, but you well understood my message. - and laughed once more making me feel intimidated.

- I'm sorry, I think I got you a little bit wrong. - I said as I smiled nervously.

- A little bit? I was dying of fear that someone might see us.

-Yes, I realized in your face and in your movements that you died of beautiful fear. - I felt that my joke was somewhat heavy, but between her and me, and even more so after what happened, there was great confidence. I finally managed to win her a fight, she fell quiet and I noticed that at first, she felt sorry for my comment immediately took me by the hand again and we continued walking towards the hotel. There were some clothing stores and before I took the elevator to get to the room, I asked him to enter one and choose a tie to debut in the presentation.

- You didn't bring a tie, then what are you coming for? - once again her jokes intimidated me.

- Of course, I brought, but I want to wear something that you have chosen so I will feel that you will be with me all the time.

- Well, I'll be with you all the time, or aren't you going to let me into the presentation? It's public, isn't it? Would you dare take me out? - once again I was overwhelmed with questions that made me red.

- I mean having you with me around, stuck to my chest all the time. - For the first time my words left her silent, so she immediately walked into that boutique and pulled my hand.

- This is the least ugly of all. -I saw her with a surprise face. - because you want more if there are few options here and we have to get ready to leave, apart I think it combines your suit if it is navy blue as you say, because then men have a completely different definition of the shades of us women. – She chose a fuchsia tie that I would never have chosen, but if she liked it, I would obviously wear it.

We went into the room to bathe quickly and prepare for the presentation of my book. We both hesitated to enter the shower if we would do it together or if we would do it separately, although we were shaking from the nerves she was causing me and more having little clothes I told her to shower together to save time that she agreed to and immediately stripped away the rest of the clothes she was wearing while I was doing the same.

Hugging it while the warm water flowing through our body was an indescribable feeling, really the time saving was just a pretext because it took several minutes there enjoying the relevant benefits of a bath with hot water.

As I longed for that bathroom to have a tub so I could rest hugging without having my legs shaking because of the double strength I had to do when Standing by the stress of having her around, outside of that, it was an excellent moment, we even had a long time to joke for a while there.

- I'll ask you about your new novel to see what you answer.

- Amy don't be like that, it will make me more nervous than I am now to know that you will be there in front of me.

- Mmm, you can't stand anything.

We laughed and started the ritual of dressing appropriately for the event, she went into the room to get dressed and I started to go over and over again all the likely questions of the attendees of the event and to review by text, all the details of such an important moment or for me, the appetizers, the guests, the room, the presenters, the printed books for sale, the supporting work units, the minutes of duration of each presenter, the wireless microphones.

It was almost an hour and she wasn't out; my mind didn't give credit to how it could take so long to get fixed. I got up from the slightly desperate armchair to knock on the door and when my hand was just two centimeters away from making contact with the wood, the door magically opened, which I saw dazzled, her hair straight, her white cheeks with freckles , her lips painted with that intense red lipstick that fascinated me, her gaze shining together with earrings the color of her eyes, a black dress glued to the knee, sexy and at the same time formal for my presentation and her smile telling me let's go!

Chapter 12

I was too nervous on that freezing Friday, not only because of the presentation of my book but because of Amy's presence in the front row of the event. If only having her around, my body would shudder and stutter or stumble through the nerves of feeling its essence, how I was going to contain my nerves of having to expose in front of it.

As I spoke I felt her tender look stalking me, in three moments of the presentation I crossed gaze with her and was fascinated by that attentive way with which I watched as every word came out of my lips, but I was also distracted and it was the only three times that I mumbled and had to review my notes something unusual in me, the first time I felt sorry, but when I discovered the way I looked at myself, the next two times I turned to see her were shorter, I preferred to observe that look and not worry about make me wrong one more time.

The bad news is that when I noticed that look that not only denoted interest, but a mixture of passion and admiration was like a little girl watching a magic show. My participation was about to end, and I would stop enjoying that feeling of her gaze. I just had magic in my words, out there I didn't know what to do with having it in front of me. We finished the presentation and there were some questions from the audience that fortunately filled the place that wasn't very big. Everything had gone excellent by removing my three mistakes that in an event of this kind that does not count much but the call and what I managed to transmit as an author to their readers, people want to see one of their favorite authors and I was happy to have several readers is when I didn't think I was that well known. I was scared and a little afraid at the same time when I saw her raise her hand and ask for the microphone to comment on something. I was eager to know what your doubts were or your impressions of my book or presentation.

She took among her delicate hands that had dawned on my chest; the wireless microphone intended to answer the questions of the attendees.

- What inspires you to write, JuanMa?

Her question drove me crazy, millions of ideas passed through my head in a second and it took me a few seconds to articulate some word, the fiercest questions of the media that day had not caused a dent as she had done in that instant.

- Hey! - I stuttered a little before I could respond - you could say that, - I calmed down and untied the knot of the tie that was suffocating me.- the inspiration depends on each writer, what motivates him, some are motivated by some beautiful natural landscape or magnificent created by man, others symbol of a great love past or present, others love to write in situations of emotional crisis such as when they feel a lot of pain or sadness, I have particular discovered that I write because I look in every story for that perfect woman, ideal, with which I can develop each of those stories that my mind creates. To this day I had fantasized in hundreds of stories with that ideal woman, reincarnating with her as in my novel "Always you", traveling in time as in my work "Yesterday", transcending our love with technology as in "Digital" inventing a story of romantic sci-fi, with a mysterious love as in "The Myth of aleph", reaching the greatest follies for love as in "Deja Vu" having a sick and erotic love as in "Psychoaffaire" first and second part, which is the work that we present this day here.

To this day I discovered that I had idealized a woman who in theory did not exist, because she combined all the qualities that I like in a woman, especially that of being pleased just by being with her. Today, September 29, 2019, my muse's dream materialized in a woman, and that woman is you.- most of the attendees were tendered to hear that words and an exclamation of admiration came out in unison, she let out a couple of tears that dried immediately thinking that you would not notice them but I did.- now I do not know if having discovered the Beatriz Viterbo, the Laura Santomé, the Aura of my novels, I can have the same creativity and imagination, perhaps today reaching my room having in front of me the keyboard of the computer does not come out anything, ideas have finished but has started a real love and not novel for me.

A monumental round of applause stoked the little place, and she couldn't stop crying until we left the place.

Signing a world of autographs was a pain to be with her, although that was the part of my life as a writer that filled me with life, to see the smile of each of my readers to enjoy what my hands could write and my mind to create , it is almost like spawning a baby in every work and seeing it conceive, gestate, being born, growing up and having a life that generates many joys.

    - Apart from being a great writer you are a very handsome man. - was a reader's comment when signing her copy of Psychoaffaire, she was very beautiful and of a similar age to mine, I can't deny that she was too attractive and I was tempted to talk a little more with her to get to know some personal details, but immediately par a soldier guarding his territory.

- And it is all mine, as he expressed in his presentation. - Amy crossed into the midst of us, and with much subtlety and understanding the indirect that elegant lady answered.

- I know, you must be very flattered. - stood in front of her in such a way that women reunite sumptuously. - Any woman would melt with her words. - the fang that gives the age in his comment apart from leaving Amy alone also launched a voracious hidden offensive to leave that flame on. They watched each other look at each other before fighting to the death, but they still put a feint, friendly smile to slowly walk away.

- You don't have to be so rude to respond; we will lose readers Amy; she was just trying to be nice.

- You will lose all the necessary readers, but you do not walk away from me this weekend not even a second that is clear to you.

That intense way of defending what she said to her that I belonged to her on the one hand frightened me, but on the other I liked that she cared so much about me, at the end of the day, no woman had defended me that way in my life.

We stayed until the last guest was removed to hold a small feedback meeting with the event organizers and evaluate the event indicators.

Near midnight we were finally able to leave the place and walk along that bridge that crosses the river holding hands, in an intense cold. We pass through the three enclosures that are almost one after the other. Paul Brown Stadium, where the Cincinnati Bengals play, we imagine the breathtaking view of the river from an armchair. Coincidentally they played that Sunday, she searched the internet for tickets to the match, I was fascinated to see live any kind of sport and even more so if it was the most popular in the USA, it should be simply a must-see show.

- Do I buy them? - asked me with an emotion that made me predict that I was doing it by creating a memory with me and not so much because I was a fan of football.

- Do you like this sport?

- I don't understand it, but if you explain it to me, I will enjoy it a lot. The truth is, I only watch the superbowl and the half-time show.

With that spontaneous and pleasant answer accompanied by that usual smile he once again thrilled my night of joy.

- That's it, they're the cheapest, but it was the only tickets available, we already have to do on Sunday.

- How? I will give you the money, tell me how much it was, and I'll give you my share. - I tried to remove my wallet from the back bag of my trousers to provide the part of my ticket, although my intention at first was, if I attended, I invite her to it and not the other way around.

-No. - put his serious face as a joke. - It is my gift to the best writer in the world for having made a perfect presentation.

I didn't say anything more about it, I was even tempted to ask the time to know what time we should have breakfast on Sunday, but I forgot the thing and continued to walk hand in hand with it, I could really do that in any circumstance, but feel the fresh and icy wind coming from the river on my cheeks and watching her honey-color hair wave gave her a deeper, more nostalgic feeling perhaps.

We passed the stadium of the legendary Cincinnati Reds, she confessed to me that it was the favorite team of her father who had passed away seven years ago, said that her father traveled to Cincinnati, had several postcards and photos of him in her room; enjoying baseball with the river as a backdrop, the last time he promised to accompany him to the next occasion and that's when he passed away. At that moment she was pensive, I think more for realizing that before she met me, she had wanted to be in this place and had not remembered it until that moment.

She was also a big fan of baseball, which was understandable, in the Pacific and more in Sinaloa people love baseball, her team in the Pacific League were the Guasave Cotton men where her grandfather once played, and when I asked her why she was a Reds fan , she told me that when she played in the Cotton salons her best friend managed to play for Cincinnati and that's why she visited him many times, although she died not very big her grandfather continued to attend the games and sometimes came to visit her family.

    - That's it!

    - What?

    - We already have tickets to get to know the stadium, it is more I bought three tickets at last that were much cheaper than those of football, so that in the seat next to yours is your grandfather accompanying us wherever he is.

I thought it would be a nice touch and I also expected a little his reaction, he let go of crying on my shoulder thanking that detail, we already had a whole weekend planned to do and we just had to walk a few blocks from the hotel to enjoy great shows world-class,

I no longer thought of attending the writers' conference. My priority was to take advantage of those days with her.

We walked a little further, I was able not to let go at any time from the hands, next to the Reds baseball stadium was the Arena where concerts were held and the Cyclones, the city's hockey team, played. There were a lot of people around so we felt he had left and so he was, I told him to buy her a beer while we watched the game and she agreed.

That hockey game was halfway and we didn't understand anything we were seeing just drank beer, we ate nachos, some delicious hotdogs, we talked about any nonsense and when people shouted excited goal we would get up too ovation the score even if we didn't have the slightest idea of what was happening in the match, we would bring our party apart, one where anything made us smile, until we saw a player fall that is the most common thing crashing on the ice in rather than cause us an exclamation of concern as the public made us burst into laughter.

We didn't even know how the game ended, but we inferred that we had won because people came out happy and creating songs from their team, we left the venue by the main entrance that overlooked a big avenue and Asked if I wanted to have dinner and told me not to , I just wanted to get to the hotel to rest and for me as her slave that was that weekend to please her in everything she said and So I did.

Chapter 13

I ordered a bottle of champagne to toast, strawberries and a gouda cheese, charged Amy from the entrance of the room to lying in bed gently, gently removed her shoes, her feet were frozen by the cold of the night, and then I continued with her dress , the earrings and accessories to make her more comfortable, uncovering the bottle and the cork fell on his feet, I poured a drink for both of us, we gave him a sip and with my teeth I lifted the cork and pushed him away from the bed as he kissed his ankles until he reached his crotch bit gently and sucking to the limit, there I stayed for a while she said nothing and well she didn't, I just heard some nice sounds, which made me feel like never before in my life, with the strength of the world to get her to be sublimated before me.

I kissed her many times on every part of her body, enjoying every fraction of a second with her, took her to the balcony with the light off and there seeing the whole city at our feet, I made love to her, she with her back to me, both looking at the wonderful illuminated city.

The time when she was in contact with me seemed to stop, though she was taking her course fiercely.

We both fell for gave up when touching the hotel's soft bed after that exhausting but pleasurable exercise, which made me feel relaxed, even though I was tired and ecstatic I couldn't sleep just watching his body lying there on the bed on one side of me.

Dawn that Saturday slowly for me when I felt the first flashes of dawn warm my eyelids. The cold was still intense at that time, so we didn't want to get out of bed and just feel the cold rubbing of our feet and how they warmed very slowly on contact and then cool again a few minutes after separating and then performing the same ritual. And even more so because my feet were almost ice for touching the wood on the floor as I got up to make you a cup of fresh coffee.

We decided to have breakfast right there on the bed anything we found on the menu and get up until the time of attending the baseball game; we made love twice.

I didn't like the idea of getting used to living my days like this, because they were too perfect and happy, but I knew that on Monday morning this dream would end.

We dress comfortably, jeans and tennis, to go to the Cincinnati Reds game. We walked down that crowded street of bars and restaurants, which becomes pedestrian during games, seeing red shirts everywhere and all sorts of Reds accessories, we arrived at the main entrance where there was a metal representation of a batter and a box, we both automatically pulled out our mobile phone to take a selfie together and in the background the fixed hairdressers there, she cried for a moment after taking those pictures where her father was photographed years ago and promised to take her to that stadium to repeat that simple photo of remembrance but next to it.

The match lasted just over five hours because there were extra-innings, we happy drinking, hugging, enjoying the wonderful scenery that represented sitting on the highest floor of the stadium with a beautiful sun illuminating the river. At first the heat was evident because I was directly exposed to the sun, but two hours later, at sunset, the icy wind cooled their cheeks and I warmed them with my lips.

The Reds won with a home run in the 11th inning and left the Pittsburgh Pirates lying down, we sat there hugging to the horizon until they started to turn off some stadium lights and we left the place step by step slowly without saying nothing just feeling next to each other, on the way out we decided to go to the souvenir shop to buy a cap just like it for both of us.

The instant we were holding hands, I heard that classic the Cars, "Drive".

"Who's gonna pay attention to your dreams…"

That simple phrase summed up what I began to desire every moment with her, to be on the lookout for all dreams, my God! I started thinking like a teenager in love and I was terrified at times that idea, when it is likely that for her this was just a beautiful adventure.

We walked along the edge of the creek as we looked at the different sculptures along the way, she stopped to play that giant piano articulated with her feet and performed that beautiful tango that was my favorite but at that moment I forgot her name, for that moment moments it was freezing my skin, more than the cold wind, to think that every hour that passed was an hour less to be with her, that I would lose her forever on the early Monday when she boarded that flight to Houston, to meet with her friend and forget the fantasy we lived , and that for her it was perhaps just a different experience with an older man from whom she would easily forget. I was stunned with every chord.

I was tormented by that nonsense when she hugged me at the end of the melody.

-If I had the heart...- I began to hum very slightly some parts of the chorus of that song.

- The same one I lost...- her voice really was a balm to my ears; I just sang out of tune.

- If I forgot the one that yesterday, I destroyed it and I could love you

- I would embrace your illusion, to mourn your love. - stopped playing and we hugged.

- It's my favorite tango, Amy.

- Mine too, we should learn to tango.

- I think it's a great idea, someday we will, I don't think it's that complicated.

We arrived at the hotel room, made love and slept hugs all night. I woke up in the early morning to drink some water and sat in front of the bed watching every detail of it, now I had to add one more quality to its perfection, its exquisite voice and its talent for the piano. How it was possible that that perfection made woman was in those moments with me, someone who had no more quality than writing fantasies that grew in my head, I thought it was a dream because my best fantasy was becoming an unforgettable reality.

So much I thought I lay next to her rubbing her legs with mine and hugged her tightly all night, although she unconsciously tried to get out I would come back repeatedly all night to settle as close to her, it was a pleasant struggle that lasted until the Dawn.

I woke up early, but I didn't stop the bed to keep hugging her, waited more than an hour for her to come back to herself and realize that I was staring at her face in her sleep.

- What will we do today?

- Try to conquer the world, Pinky. - We both laughed with that nonsense that was a classic phrase of an old cartoon.

- Today we get the football game, remember.

- It's true, let's have some breakfast in front of the river and from there we enter the game, shall we? - obviously I loved that she proposed something, it was a symptom that she enjoyed being with me.

- I find it an excellent beautiful idea. By the way, you are horrible to sleep with, all night I've been hugging myself and you're getting sloping.

- It's just that I detested to sleep like this, excuse me if I accidentally gave you a knee. – said as he blushed.

- Don't worry it was mild.

I lay on his legs and there I began to imagine that moment when we would first attend a stadium to watch a football game.

Chapter 14

We were getting ready to attend the football game, a whole new experience for her and me. We had heard so many things about the excitement of this sport, the most popular in the United States, that we could not miss the opportunity to live it together for the first time.

From the departure of the local team was impressive the deafening sound that was heard from the hobby and music at full volume. That classic "The Verb," Bittersweet Symphony, sounded deafening, as more than a hundred orange-hulled players entered the field one by one.

Some things of the match were not understood; however, we really enjoyed the intensity of the fans by scoring the representative team of the city where we were living this odyssey that I wished never ended.

Those three hours spent like water between screams, hugs, kisses, popcorn, beer, hotdogs, nerves and a lot of happiness.

- JuanMa! JuanMa, wake up!

- What happened?

- You fell asleep.

- I'm sorry **I was beautiful, are you** ready?

- Yes, let's go to breakfast as we left and from there to the game.

We walked along the avenue that led directly to the stadium and the river, we found before the stadium a place that looked very rich, it was a Belgian franchise and as I brought the wish of waffles I proposed to her for breakfast there and she accepted. We sat at a table on the terrace of the place from where we could see not only the sea but also the majestic stadium of the Bengali, we ordered coffee and waffles for both while we looked around the details of the game, only that there was a somewhat strange detail.

I found it strange that just three hours after starting the game, there was still no movement nearby, in Veracruz when the Soccer team plays they even close several avenues before and open the stadium doors six hours before, but here the property was still observed closed, which I was going to tell Amy but I thought we were in the first world surely no traffic problems because the avenues and accesses are enough and people arrive almost just on time because all the places are numbered not like in Mexico that although are numbered people sit wherever they do not respect that order.

She started cutting pieces of my waffles and giving them to her in the mouth, that gesture made her look tender and more affectionate than she had been so far.

- Looks very quiet around the state, don't you think?

- I thought the same thing a while ago and that only two hours before the start, maybe everyone arrives with a few minutes to go. Although it would be wise to approach to know which entrance we will access before it fills up with people and we must walk slower.

- I find it perfect, in fact, I'm done with breakfast, so when you like we go.

I paid the bill and walked a block to one of the entrances and the property was still empty, it was strange not to see the trucks of the food and beer suppliers arriving hours early to have their products ready at game time. The silence around it was no longer normal.

I asked her to check the e-tickets on his mobile phone to check the date and time of the match, probably the time of day of the event was different from what we had understood.

We didn't find anything different on the ticket, so I decided to open the NFL page online to see if the game had been rescheduled or changed schedules, but no, the game would appear ready in an hour and twenty-seven minutes.

We sat down for a few moments to chat on one of the little benches outside the stadium while we waited to see someone to ask about the event. Strangely, not a soul passed by.

- This is really weird, isn't it?

- Yes, because even the external modules are not open.

- Do we wait?

- Well we wait, but if we take a walk around the whole property to see if there is anyone who can inform us.

We walked as we continued to talk about the live sporting events we had witnessed throughout our lives.

- I was at the World Cup in Russia, Ricardo invited me and because we went to the games of the national team until we were eliminated.

- I have only watched the World Cup in Mexico 86, my father took me as a child to watch the game of Mexico against Germany and weeded out of that match because we lost in series of penalties, joined the Colombian referee who annulled us a legitimate goal in the second half. I also had the pleasure of attending the World Cup in Germany with my father and it was something of a revenge because I was in the semi-final when all the Germans wept when Roberto del Piero and the Italian national team eliminated them in overtime. It was vibrant at first to see the stadium full and the chants supporting the Germans and then watch them cry down the halls as I did at the University Stadium in Monterrey when we were eliminated, divine justice.

- For not so divine because they were champions in Russia.

- Well at least that consolation was left to win on Russian soil in football because in the first and second world wars they were worth. -

- I also love watching live sports, that emotion that is felt in the stadiums when the local team plays is something that chills the skin, that deafening sound is exciting.

- That's why I'm fascinated by live shows, although let me confess that the most deafening sound I've ever heard in my life is not at a football match or some sport. The most impressive sound that my ears have felt is the one that made me vibrate when I took my niece to see the concert of her favorite group.

- Well, what did they go to see the Beatles, or which group can generate such a scenario?

- You're going to make fun of me when I tell you the name. - I said sorry.

- Let it go, leave the mystery.

- There was no one to take her so I had to sacrifice myself to accompany her to see the Jonas Brothers, you can't imagine the cry of thousands of teenagers, it was a little rare I came out of that concert.

- What you fell under, I hope you don't think of seeing something like this here in Cincinnati.

- Not as you think. - we made a full return to the stadium and it was at that moment that I knew why there was no one in the stadium.

Chapter 15

- Section 107, Row 28 Seats 17 and 18, Atlanta Falcons vs. Cincinnati Bengals, Sunday September 30 1:00 PM, Mercedes-Benz Stadium. Baby, we're standing at Paul Brown Stadium.

- What about that? it's today at one p.m. the party.

- Yes, but not in this stadium. - her face blushed and she fell silent and with the attitude of a scolded child, I kept laughing to remember the emotion with which I woke up that day to watch that match with her, even more than that day I did not attend congress so that I could be with her all day and enter the stadium early.

- Sorry, I thought the game was here in Cincinnati.

- I also feel like an idiot - I said laughing - let's not worry you're just a damn game the important thing is that we're together, well we can see it in some bar or better even let's go to the Reds Stadium to watch the last game of this series against Pittsburg...- she didn't give credit to what we had gone through, yet it was an anecdote; one of those that comes under our secret because it's obvious that we would never tell anyone, was to expose our stupidity.

- Cost $250 each ticket. - she insisted even lamenting.

- Don't worry baby, it's something material, what's more, I pay for tickets to the Reds game. - Her countenance changed, but she still felt uneasy, more than worried about the money she had invested fruitlessly, she seemed sorry for not consenting to something she had done for me.

It was a delight to enjoy the Reds game with her again and that's how I made him feel to forget that football ticket thing, which inside instead of sadness made me so laughing at our mistake.

We left the stadium which was only six blocks from the hotel and on the corner we saw a Belgian food franchise where they sold craft beers; we went in and sat on the terrace to watch the sunset, I chose one that had 12 degrees of alcohol for her, it was our last night together so I had decided to make her lose her mind so I could hug her all night without her being able to walk away as usual and have her at leisure for me. She drank it as if it were water and when she got up to the bar bathroom wobbled a little, she collided with a chair from the next table until she finally went to the bathroom.

It took her a little while to get back and when he did he ordered another beer the same as I, refused because it was already something taken, I wanted to have it accessible but not unconscious, so I ordered a very light one.

- What time does your flight depart?

- At nine o'clock in the morning, I must be at seven at the airport, so I have to leave at six o'clock at the hotel at the latest.

- Perfect, I'll set my alarm at five o'clock to make you a coffee and order a taxi to wait for us at six. - I told her as I set my phone alarm at that time.

She notoriously changed her countenance of joy for one of sadness, it was evident the fall of her eyebrows when something did not make her feel good and the tone of her voice more gravely, she confirmed.

- We will say goodbye to the night before bed, I will go alone to the airport. I don't want a sad farewell, I want to remember this moment forever in a happy way without so much drama or startling, so I'll say goodbye to you with a kiss on the cheek when you sleep.

- How you think we'll do that; I'll leave you every last corner that I'll be allowed to do. What's more, if you like I can take the same flight with you to Houston and from there return to Mexico, please tell me yes.

- JuanMa, it's been three wonderful days, maybe one of the best of my life but I have to go back to reality, you have no idea of the emotion that gave me to meet you and I don't mean the fact that I greeted you in the book store, but the pleasure of knowing every intimate detail of you , you've made me feel so many things that it's a danger for both of us to get on with it, haven't you noticed our surroundings, I think I look like the 42-year-old and not you.

- It is not a matter of maturity, never in three days had someone been able to make me feel what you have in my whole life and now you ask me to be mature, I would cry to beg you if necessary.

- Don't make it harder, we just need to both get back to our world.

I felt that immense sadness of when my heart was broken on previous occasions. How could I say those words, what if my world was her, which was quite likely since no woman in my more than four decades of existence had made me feel what I felt for her, of being every second by her lips , maybe that's why I was still single at this age because I'd been looking for someone to do the same crazy things I do, especially to make them tangible.

However, I couldn't violate her decision, if she did it was for something, maybe she didn't feel the same way about me, maybe I was just a test for her, and then I was just going back into her boyfriend's arms, maybe It was just me who proved that all she wanted was to be with him. Or maybe I went to the one who could compare him to him and finally decided the best option for her.

I was martyred to think that, but I couldn't do anything else, I could only offer her the few years that were left over from my life, but if she didn't want her reasons I would have. So, I was strong and said to everything I was.

I convinced her to walk along the riverbank, to make the most of the time next to her, I didn't want the night to end and more with that fresh fog that made her stay in my arms at every step as a necessity. Every movement in the second hand made me feel in a scene of a death row inmate listening to the ticking of the clock, waiting for the moment of his next execution.

We walked into a bar that was on that avenue that closed on weekends so the youngsters could have fun next to the Reds Stadium.

She laughed every time I started a song from the eighties, and I saw myself getting excited and then seeing her smiling I felt sorry.

I had nothing special, only that made me feel like nobody, it was something totally difficult to explain, in the simplicity to do anything I was perplexed showing incredible intelligence.

At night his honey-colored eyes were no longer like the sky bathed in sunrays, they were dark maple color, that serious tone, that tone that made me remember the sea of my city at night.

- Where would you like to be right now and with whom?

- I would love to stay a few hours in my city, in Coatzacoalcos, in those brief lapses that it takes the sun to set and give me every day the most beautiful passage I have ever known, until I met your smile, so at this time what I would most wish for is the sunset over the sea of my land and the hill of St. Martin in the background.

- Wow! Sounds like it's a very beautiful place.

- I don't know if it is, but it fascinates me, I have traveled all over the world and I have not found a landscape that can be matched, the Swiss Alps, the Chinese wall, the Grand Canyon, the Perito Moreno glacier. With the difference that I'd like to be there watching the sunset next to that woman who made me vibrate like no one in life.

- Your ex-girlfriend? Why aren't you with her now?

- Who has made me feel what no one, is you.

She hugged me more tenderly than ever and we both melted into a strong hug as she cried and said not to make it any harder. At that moment I felt like when a woman is going to leave you and asks you not to beg her not to make you suffer anymore and not make her feel uncomfortable, so I did not without first saying something to her ear.

- My dream would be that one day we were you and I together in that place.

- Don't tell me those things please.

And she cried again now more intense and difficult to control, so we were for minutes and I didn't say any more, we just walked back to the hotel.

- How will the novel be titled?

- I have no idea, what name would you give it?

- Rareness or coincidences.

- You hear either of those two names, I would put you, an indescribable smile.

- Does it fascinate you so much?

- Yes, and more when you're about to, you know, finish.

- Seriously, stop saying those things that I barely.

- That's how I realize when you're done, when I hear and see your smile enjoy it.

- Since we are in the session stage, how many women have you been with?

- I won't tell you, you don't want to know.

- Why?

- Because you will think that you were as important as that number of women, but for me only you are important, it is more I would only have been with you in my life, even if it sounds trite and amazing. - What about you? How many men have you been with?

- Do you think I'm a nymphomaniac or what? - Her sense of humor was unbelievable. - Only with my boyfriend.

- Yes, I imagine that it must be very measurable to let you come alone, I would not neglect you for a second of my sight.

- Really? What a sexist.

- Call me whatever you want, but I wouldn't stray a second away from you. - we stop to see the stream for the last time before climbing the staircase that overlooks the hotel and losing sight of it. - What will you do after completing the master's degree?

- I don't know. Chances are I'll go back to my homeland and work with my father in his company. What are you going to do going back to Mexico?

- Write our story, publish it, win a Nobel for it and at that moment go and look for you to the place where you are to show you what we achieve together.

- The idea doesn't sound bad, I like it, although a Nobel doesn't give it for a better novel any prize you get you teach me and tell me that we won it together to feel important?

- Deal done.- She reached out my hand and squeezed it tightly closing that deal and kissed me very passionately so I responded to the degree of lowering her pants and there in that dark street having the view of the creek I lowered the closure of my trousers and made the biggest madness of my life, when we realized it was already inside it, we both trembled with the nerves of being there and someone discovering us, a second later a car bent in the corner caught up with its lights and we immediately separated.

We couldn't stand the laughter of our follies, we kept walking fast as we settled our clothes until we arrived hotel.

I took off her clothes with difficulty because of everything we had drunk, I caressed the skin of every part of her body with the fingertips, it was the last time I was going to have her next to me. So, I took advantage of until the last minute, tried not to fall asleep so I could say goodbye to her and hug her for the last time and maybe convince her to see us again. But she did her best to make me surrender in her arms.

Instantly I first opened my eyes with sunlight coming through the curtain of the window, my flying mind connected and I looked for it immediately, I jumped up to observe the time and know if I still had the possibility of reaching it at the airport contrary to her will.

Chapter 16

Unfortunately, it was nine o'clock in the morning, in the worst case the flight had been delayed anyway I would already be in the last waiting room where only passengers can access it.

I screamed furiously, feeling my stomach burning with courage and helplessness, unintentionally began to cry, and watched it start raining outside with cloudy skies as I wept from his departure.

I wanted to mark him thousands of times to find out if she'd made it to the airport well, but I was sad in her decision to finish that adventure in that instant. I couldn't stay locked up any longer, I felt like I was choking on those four walls without her. So, I sheltered and went for a walk again on the same path I walked next to her.

Every instant when I had the opportunity I would turn to see my mobile phone to check if I had received any messages from her, but no, first I thought I should be traveling, so it was time until it was impossible for me to keep traveling, had nightfall, my curiosity and desperation for not knowing anything overcame me, so back in the room I went into her Facebook account to review her latest posts, I felt a "millennial" using social media to spy on people, even though I didn't have her friend I could recent contributions. Seeing the first was enough...

"What a pleasant surprise!"

And a picture of her with her boyfriend who apparently just that day had come to see her in Houston.

On the one hand, I felt a great pain in my chest, but on the other hand a great relief to know that she was fine and that she was happy.

It was the logical thing, it should not surprise me, she had only been a shooting star, which unfortunately left a trail on me, which at the time seemed very complex to forget.

I felt very uneasy, my mind constantly betrayed me, and I imagined the lips of that guy kissing Amy's and my body was buddy, it was furious until I wanted to blow everything around. And as much as I tried to change my thoughts I was assaulted every second an image of them from a kiss that made me go into anger to imagine them making love, putting their filthy hands on my Amy, were moments of great anger and confusion that did not cease and not I could relax.

I began to feel that I was suffocating locked in that room just thinking about her and what I would be doing in those moments with Ricardo, so I had to go out and breathe fresh air that would help me relax and calm the desire I had to run to see her and get rid of as it gave rise to that guy.

I was really not calm, for very short moments I felt liberated by not having already that nice pressure of having to do everything right and plan everything perfect so that she would be happy, but the rest of the time it was a pain to think of her, where would she be , doing what? I was getting angry to the slightest sound of flying a fly near me. My head could burst at any moment, so I perceived it because of how hot I felt inside every time I imagined it with it, or worse my destructive mind imagined it with some other man and went crazy irritating every one of my billions of neurons . That's why I thought the only option was to bewitch them.

I entered that cozy place of Belgian origin where the night before we had drunk craft beer. I ordered the same drink as that day and took my personal computer out of the backpack. I started writing the end of my novel about our story imagining that she was sitting in front of me at the time, I could even swear that I felt her breathing. I was sitting right at the same table and every word he wrote his smile appeared spontaneously and inspired me to write more.

After drinking that beer that made her stagger, I re-imagined it and felt that it was almost real, even though it looked paranoid, I felt the table move like that day when she accidentally hit it when she came back from the bathroom.

Damn, what was happening to me, she had gone into my mind and I had opened the doors to her without contemplation.

I ordered that same dinner to disrupt my mind and to be able to almost give a pleasant ending to this story that had had a real disastrous ending.

I put some music on that device that simulated an old schooler and chose after romantic songs to inspire me.

I know I saw myself very idiotizing standing for a while in the space between the bar and the first tables of the bar, holding my beer while I remembered that it was right where my feet were when I kissed it passionately the night before , I knew because in that duel there was a sticker from a football team.

I drank all night until my tired old body could no longer hold, so as I could I walked to the hotel staggering along those five blocks, until I finally arrived.

I drank liters of water from the faucet at the entrance of the hotel hoping that this would lessen the effect of alcohol on me, and that the abundant hydration would lessen the discomfort I would surely have in the morning.

I woke up with a terrible hangover, yet the remedy of drinking a lot of water before bed, was already half a day when I heard someone knocking on the door, I immediately stood up and dressed up with the first thing I found.

Chapter 17

I hadn't finished opening the door of the room and I slammed over her hugging her.

- Thank you, thank you for staying with me, Amy. – I said it while shedding some tears of emotion.

- I couldn't just leave like that, for me these days too they were unique, and I felt something I had never felt.

I kept thanking her again and again for allowing me to spend more time with her.

- What will we do beautiful?

- How can we know if this relationship is truly unique and eternal?

- For there is only one way to know, in the long run all relationships deteriorate, becoming monotonous, however, when there is a connection, a spark that always ignites and brightens every word from one to the other, as long as there is be a couple forever.

- What will happen if after a while we discover that it is not the relationship, we both seek?

- Nothing will happen, just if we're not made to be together everyone will make their life and now.

- Okay, let's try it, how long will we be together?

- My trip to Houston would last three weeks so we have that time to live together and be able to figure out if we're made to be together.

- I think it's perfect, where do you want to go today on our last day in Cincinnati?

- We go through all the art galleries that are along the center, here is a map that indicates where each one is located, there are eleven just around.

-Come on, hey, but I don't understand that picture on Facebook you posted where you were already in Houston with your friend and your boyfriend. - I said with some trepidation to think that it was a dream that my mind was creating, or that my comment might annoy you.

- It's from last year right on these dates, when we accompanied Mafer to know the school where I was going to study and the city, it appeared to me in my memories when I was at the airport and instead of making me feel happy with that memory, I was saddened to think that I would have liked or that you were the one in the picture.

- Thank you, Amy. - I hugged it and squeezed it very hard.

Our first discussion was about her return ticket, she insisted on paying for it and I as a gentleman, apart from being left to me, insisted on covering the payment.

Since we didn't reach a consensus she was upset and threatened not to travel with me. I had no choice but to access it. Sometimes women are too stubborn, and Amy was too stubborn, she was one of her traits that made me crazy, but I also understood that it was because of her age and her short experience in the life that she behaved in that way. I wanted with all my strength to mold her to my way of being or at least help her mature a little faster.

The first four days in Coatzacoalcos, were perfect, the first place I took her immediately to land was to the beach. We stopped at a liquor store to buy a bottle of wine and enjoy it watching the sunset. She loved the view from the taxi to the hill of San Martín.

- It's magical. "She remarked as she lay her head on my shoulder and sighed, I watched her, and she was serene and happy at that beautiful moment. I felt I could spend my life with her.

We arrived at the beach and asked the taxi to wait for us so that we could go down to enjoy the sunset. Immediately she sat in the sand, I was surprised that she did not mind sitting down and that her skin was exposed to getting dirty, she had that way of being that she cared nothing more than to enjoy the moment. I opened the bottle and when we forgot to buy glasses, we had to drink directly from it. Amy took her between her delicate, beautiful hands and toasted.

- For us and the future together, always together.

I felt like I was living in a dream, that woman with the most beautiful smile in the universe thought of having a future with me, a simple writer older than her and an average physique, nothing special. We drank and she leaned on the sand by putting her head on my thigh. I took several pictures of her in that position. I was tempted to make love to her there, but there were a lot of runners flying past us and I didn't want to expose her to a bad time just because I couldn't control my desire for her.

- JuanMa, promise me something. – asked me to get out of my lustful thoughts.

- Tell me baby.

- Promise me that whatever happens I will always be your muse, your inspiration and that in your mind I will always be the perfect woman.

- I promise you. - I responded with the thought that this promise was over, I already had a thousand stories in my mind that I wanted to write, and they were all for and for her.

- I promise to always be your number one fan.

- Well baby, let my mother not hear you say that because she won't like it. - I said laughing.

- I want to meet her. - She said as she sat down and looked me straight in the eye with that devastating smile drawn on her face. I laughed, it was a trick to convince me and I hugged her tightly as she laughed without being able to stop. She was adorable even when she was trying to manipulate me.

- I'll see what I can do to get you to meet my parents. - I answered as soon as I **could stop laughing and** she thanked me with a tender kiss on my forehead.

As soon as we got to my house she fell into the room and I didn't want to wake her, I started to mark my family to organize a meal where everyone was, and she could meet them. I was so excited that the people most important to me could meet Amy and adore her as much as I did.

The next day I simply asked her to put on a dress to go to a magical place in my city, one of my favorite places. I drove slowly to increase the sense of mystery, she would go out the window watching the boardwalk and try to get me to tell her what our destination was, she even came to blackmail me with not having sex with me if I didn't tell her where we were going, but I didn't give in and she was wincing s of anger that they were faked. She started to see a lagoon and got excited instantly, I saw her smile and I felt satisfied, but that wasn't the surprise. I parked next to a palapa that stood by the lagoon.

- We arrived at Barrilas Baby, one of the most important tourist places of my land. – I said with great pride

- I love it, it's beautiful.

We got out of my van and I took it by the hand to walk together towards the palapa that was u restaurant, many tables were occupied, I was immediately heading to the one on the far left, there were the people who were the real surprise. When I got to the table, I stopped and made the presentations. Amy was elated to meet my parents, my younger sister and my closest friends, everyone greeted them with a kiss and an effusive hug. My mother asked her to sit next to her and then I saw Amy's face transform, I saw her play with the fingers of her hands and nervously move her leg. I loved that my mother made her nervous, that made me understand that she cared that she liked her. As the hours passed Amy relaxed until she and my mother talked as if they had known each other for years. Though on second thought, my mother has always been an angel and adored everyone. By the time the afternoon fell I decided to steal Amy for a while and took her to a hammock near the table and we lay down hugging.

- Thank you for letting me know the most important people in your life.

- Thank you for being here with me. – I answered happily, I've never been so happy in my life.

We slept for a while like that hugged, enjoying the breeze that ran and as background music the laughter and voices of the most important people in my life. My sister woke us up and I noticed her face wasn't very friendly. She asked me to help her set up some handmade things in her car that she had bought from some passing vendors. I loaded everything and walked with her to her car, she didn't talk anything too unusual about her, she's as talkative or more talkative than I am. When he got to her trunk, she opened, and I settled all her purchases inside. I decided to walk away, but she stopped me by the arm, and I turned to see her straight in the eye. I thought I had a problem and would ask me for help, I never imagined that words would come out of his mouth that would make me angry and spoil the happiness of the moment.

- Juan, I don't like your girlfriend. I've been watching her, and I don't think she's sincere. Something's hiding.

I immediately let go of her arm, a thousand things passed through my mind, how I could judge her if I hadn't spoken to her.

- You don't know her. – I replied very annoyingly

- Neither do you. Sit down and watch her and you'll see there's something wrong with her.

I didn't want to answer her anymore, I was sure jealous because she used to be the center of my attention and I used to pamper her the whole time we were together, but this afternoon all my attentions had been for Amy. I decided to put a smile on my face, although inside I was disappointed in my sister and very upset with her.

Amy didn't realize what happened and I thanked heaven for that, I didn't want to spoil her this special day.

When we got home, we took a bath together and made love, this time calmly, we were exhausted but the desire was beating strongly between us. We went to bed and fell asleep right away, I noticed that she sleeps upside down and it was that I understood why she found it so difficult to keep us hugged all night. I decided to adjust to her posture and slept a little uncomfortable but happy to have her with me. In the early morning she woke me up seducing me, wanted to make love to me and I felt like the luckiest man in the world.

The days passed quickly, for the weekend we traveled to Texistepec the place where the oldest known civilization of America, Los Olmecas, was born. For me it was an amazing trip, but she didn't enjoy it so much. During a show called "Los Morenos" the dancers dance with ropes and then whip each other with them, it's a choreography, but Amy couldn't stand it and ran out. I found her two streets later in a small coffee shop sitting with tears in her eyes, hugging her and she apologized explaining that she did not tolerate violence of any kind. I tried to explain that it was only part of a show, but she did not want to hear about it, and we went to the hotel walking hand in hand. So fragile and yet so strong, Amy sometimes seemed to be the man in the relationship being so open and out of her and at other times she was a fearful child who needed my protection. Despite that awkward moment, I felt that the trip was perfect simply because she was by my side.

The next day when I returned to Coatzacoalcos, I left her alone for a couple of hours at my house. I had decided to surprise him and prepare a romantic dinner to celebrate our relationship, short but very intense. A friend of mine helped me to borrow the city lighthouse located in the bicentennial museum, went to the best restaurant to order the best seafood, I bought several bottles of wine and put everything in a picnic basket. I bought roses, all in red and adorned the way to the little corner where we would have dinner. I came back for her and found her upset that I left her for so long, I had to beg her to agree to go out to dinner with me and after a while she agreed. When she got in the van, she took the picnic basket and wanted to open it, but I stopped it.

- Not yet baby, we will picnic, and it is part of a surprise that I have prepared for you.

She kept quiet all the way, I was exasperated by the silence, but I decided to respect her and not force her to speak. From my experience, I knew it was sometimes better to let women calm down on their own. We arrived and I helped her out of the van, took her hand to guide her and in the other I loaded the picnic basket.

- Oh my God, this is beautiful. " shouted as I saw the path of petals and candles leading us up upstairs. I smiled and kept quiet; she took my hand harder. Arriving upstairs he realized we were in a lighthouse and he burst into tears of emotion, spread kisses all over my face. - It's the most beautiful thing anyone's ever done for me. " he said as he gave me the most passionate kisses, which led us to make love there on that blanket destined for the picnic. It was a magical moment, we made love twice before we got dressed again and sat down to enjoy our picnic, the food a little cold, but it tasted delicious. At the end we made love once more and we lay down enjoying the starry sky.

Chapter 18

After the honeymoon lived those days I returned to work and she accompanied me on some occasions. The academic work that was my lifelong vocation seemed not to be what she expected. I was used to superfluous things in life.

The second week was no longer honey on flakes, the age difference was beginning to wreak havoc.

She had different expectations than mine.

I knew it because at our dinner to celebrate two weeks of meeting, with candles and wine, all night we talked about it, she very subtlety made me understand with family examples that I expected to change lifestyle, I made the same , my expectations are that I was the ideal wife not a capricious girl looking for idealistic things that went far from my current life and what I did.

Where the magic, the chemistry, the spark of that journey in which everything was perfect, had been all circumstantial and should have ended the moment she took a flight to Houston and remained the perfect story, unforgettable, idealized by both.

The last few days together became even more monotonous, that monotony that couples experience after long years of routine and knowing every detail of the other person, we were beginning to suffer just weeks after we met.

If I left her alone for a while, she'd be upset, and didn't understand that my work was as important as the relationship. That I had to meet him in order to pay for trips, dinners and all the whims that occurred to her. I didn't mind pampering her, I've always been a man who fervently believes that women should be treated like queens, but she sometimes asked for things just to ask and then I'd put them aside and never come near them again. In the evenings it was the same as always, first a sermon for having taken so long working, then the demand to go out to dinner and to end sex where she being upset told me that she punished me and just lay there without doing much , although I always felt it end. That bothered me a lot and when she noticed that my patience was about to reach her limit, then she struggled to cook me, hug me, kiss me and decided to seduce me, I would always fall, and my anger vanished. She was my weakness and we both knew it.

There was only one moment when he blew me up, I remember that day he accompanied me to my work and since we arrived, she put on a bad face, that's how it was all day. My colleagues greeted her, and she did not answer them, by the middle of the afternoon I decided to give her the keys to my van and to go home, I would return by taxi when my workday was over. When the time to get home, I decided to take a while longer, I didn't want to go back to the routine every night, I didn't want any more claims for things that were never going to change. I decided to write and so I missed the time, big mistake on my part because around eight o'clock at night I received a very annoying message.

I see that you are not interested in spending time with me, I have my suitcase ready and I bought a flight for tomorrow first thing. I'm leaving.

I tried to answer her, but Amy had already blocked me, I growled, that had been the last straw. When I got to the house, I paid the taxi driver and I didn't worry about the change, I just wanted to go in and put the cards on the table.

- Finally, you decide to arrive.

Everything was dark, but I was able to distinguish his voice coming from the room, walked without answering him and turned on all the lights.

- What's wrong with you Amy? Are you out of your mind?

Hearing that phrase, she turned into a fierce and started throwing the cushions at me.

- Crazy? You deserve not to arrive early, to leave me alone, to flirt with other women in my face! If that's being crazy, then I am and quite a lot.

- Amy calm down and talk like the adults we are.

- Are you implying that I behave like a child?

- You are a spoiled and spoiled girl who wants everything her way and if she does not do as she wants then to come the reproach, punishments and rudeness! – Exploded

- No one had insulted me in this way. – shouted

- Because you relate to kids, fuck Amy sit down and let's talk or I'm gone, and I don't sleep here today.

Faced with that threat she sat down to cry and babble, between times I heard that she said that I did not understand her and that I did not love her. I immediately realized it was a manipulative trick to make me feel bad and for me to apologize. I wasn't, I was tired of your babysitting.

- Since you don't calm down, I'll go upstairs for clothes and go to sleep at my parents' house. – I got up from a decided armchair, heartbroken but determined, I could not continue to allow so many whims in the relationship or play with me that way.

- JuanMa don't go. - she asked, and then I went back to the living room, but in the chair farthest from her.

- What's wrong with Amy? You weren't like that, I know I know you little, but I don't think you can be that unbalanced.

- I'm not crazy JuanMa, understand I didn't think you were like that either.

- Explain yourself - I asked

- No offense, but you lead a very monotonous and sometimes boring life. – that was a direct stab to my heart.

- Why do you say that monotonous and boring? " I said trying to hide my cut voice.

- I thought that as a writer you would make many presentations, we would travel to many cities, that we would go to many parties dedicated to you. I also thought you were a faithful man, but I see you flirt with all the women in your work.

At that moment my veins boiled, I felt like I didn't want to see her. The age difference was becoming too noticeable or maybe it wasn't the age difference but the education our parents had given us.

- Look Amy I will say this and do not interrupt me because if you do here the relationship ends. We're not old enough for these dramas. – she wanted to talk, but I clean her with her eyes, and she fell silent. – Number one, my life is this if you like it well and if not also, I love my job and I love writing, I will not leave my job to lead a more banal life of parties, travel and autograph signatures. You want to go out, go ahead and do it, I'm not going to stop you. With me is not party every weekend or trips every time, with me it is something more stable, perhaps boring for you, but stable and very desirable for someone who wants to share his life with the person he loves. I don't need numbers or dramas almost every day, I need a partner who supports me and is with me in the good, bad and the worst. I want to have someone by my side who values the routine of going to bed to watch some series or just dine a day at home something prepared by me or requested to go. - Number two, my co-workers are my friends, almost as a family of so many years that we have been working together, I am affectionate because obviously I love them, we have all been together as a great family for years and if you are going to be rude with my friends who **are also** my co-workers, as you were today and that is why I asked you to retire, then I will not take you back to work with me. I may be in love with you, but that doesn't mean I'm going to tolerate whims and rudeness. This is my life; you take it to leave it.

She put on her face and ran up to the bedroom and locked herself in it. I heard her break something, but I didn't want to go over to find out what it was. I took the keys to my truck and went to a hotel. I didn't want my parents to find out I was having such strong problems with Amy, just so soon after we met. Surprisingly I fell asleep at the time of touching the bed.

The next morning, I went back to the house and found Amy in the living room, this time she ran to hug me and apologize for the crazy things she did. She swore she wanted to share everything with me and that he would change her attitude. Instantly a weight I didn't know was on my shoulders went away, I took a deep breath and hugged it.

As her departure drew up, we were both trying to make the other happy, the fight was still in our minds, but her early departure had made us send her to a corner as far away from our present as possible. We were trying to enjoy every moment we had together.

On the last day I **planned** a perfect dinner, with candles, wine, and on the most beautiful setting, the sunset of the city and then a starry night. The terrace of my parents' house overlooked the boardwalk and the sea, it was the perfect setting for that dinner, they had gone on a trip and lent me their house to give that surprise to Amy.

We both had so many things to say to each other, it seemed that it was only when the time was coming to get away, we felt that pressure again and brought back the best out of our relationship. So it was that night that we didn't sleep toasting with the breeze that curled the skin of his body. She wore a flowery white dress that showed the outer beauty of her legs well-turned by tennis, her gaze began to shine brighter every minute that the moon also did reflecting on her. It was a moment like us who lived in Cincinnati and the first days in Coatzacoalcos, we both wanted all our moments in life to be like this, we had the magic formula to create perfect moments in the face of the scarcity of time, but we didn't have that same formula to achieve a magical routine that would make living together day by day just as spectacular. We both knew that why we enjoyed that moment so much regardless the next morning, agreed date for your return flight.

Again at four o'clock in the morning she proposed as she bit half a grape and gave me to bite the other half directly from her lips, that I would not get up to say goodbye, that she took a taxi to the airport, now she insisted more vehemently , claimed that the pain would be more intense on this occasion when we already knew each other enough. We were no longer strangers embarking on a weekend adventure together.

I accepted once again thinking about getting up without her consent and accompanying her, but at that perfect moment I would not debate you for that.

- What will be the end of your novel?

- I can't tell you until you read it printed on a cover where we both show not in a photograph, but in two symbols or places that represent us

- There will also be a moment to decide whether I leave or stay.

- I don't know, I think it's all going to end the day you leave the airport and say goodbye to me, kissing me on the mouth thinking I'm about to sleep, but I'm just pretending I don't want to complicate your life or make you feel bad about something.

- Sounds very cowardly that ending, it should look like reality, that we risked, that we tried, that we did everything in our power to try to oxygenate that love that was born in a strange situation. I think that should be the case whatever decision you both make, you should try, otherwise the reader will tear you apart with their reviews.

- You're right, I'll figure out how to give it an entertaining ending for the reader.

- What end are you going to put on?

- I don't think we should talk about it, other than the decision is yours tomorrow, you board that plane or not. Remember, we didn't talk about it and enjoy the night.

- The night is about to end for us, it is half an hour before it is 6 am and therefore for sunrise and that we go to your house to prepare my suitcase and from there decide.

- What if I don't fall asleep this time?

- Well, you'll automatically know in that instant what happened.

- You're right.

At times I was excited to think that she would make the decision to stay and we could relive the best moments we experienced striving to improve our relationship. But also on the other I was overwhelmed by the sadness of thinking of a future with her in which the difference in ages would mean a great obstacle, together to remember that the days we had spent together had not been what we both hoped for from a relationship forever , and then I thought that the best option, although it hurt me was her departure and leave those days as unforgettable. And so, feel liberated

Once again, she managed to leave me exhausted with every kiss, with every caress, with every glass of wine, with every second that grazed my head to make me fall off and sleep in her legs.

I got up and felt the same way that that cold morning in Cincinnati, an immense pain, she was no longer, once again she had walked away me, I screamed again in pain but now I understood that that fantasy story had been circumstantial, in life there are two kinds of loves , the circumstantial that arises when there is no other option, when people find themselves emotionally unstable as in the magical story we live, both are in an ideal situation where everything goes perfectly for moments and everything walks cheerfully; and the true love that is the one that you know and know everything about that person and still love her despite her flaws, the two are a team that works equally to make the relationship work and that accepts that not everything has to be perfect always , that in the routine there is also perfection.

Knowing her was one of the things I'll never forget in my life. I lived the best days and nights of my life; I will want every day to be like that.

Chapter 19

Sadness made me sink into bed, I couldn't believe that my indecision, that my annoyance and fed-up made me not fight for it anymore. At times I wished she would knock on the door of my house and for others I was glad that there would be no more anger. I felt like a carousel of emotions unfolding and changing for the second. I didn't know when I fell asleep.

There were only a couple of hours left for her to make her way to the airport so I was going to drink a cup of coffee to scare off the dream that was beginning to beat me, when I took the cup to serve me tiredness, I was overcome.

- Amy, you chose to stay with me, I love you

I hugged her very tight.

Perhaps I wanted more to leave and free myself from the stress of fighting for her every day, however, when I passed the option of her to stay, my heart was racing pleasantly, and my stomach felt a void. Undoubtedly the emotion of her staying with me was not only greater but incomparable by so many different sensations that she provoked me.

That day I dialed the office to ask permission to miss unpaid. I was dedicated to teaching the chair of literature at the state public university. It was what I did alternatively besides writing.

We planned to go to breakfast on the top floor of that tower where you could see every penny of the sea horizon, adorned with boats seeming to float over that imaginary line dividing the sky and the sea.

We made love with a passion as in the days of our first times, perhaps by releasing the stress of never seeing each other again, I felt it because at the time of finishing we both felt a great peace and we relaxed until we fall asleep for an hour, however , I got up with a lot of energy to take advantage of that day off by his side.

I went to bathe in what she called her mother to inform her that she would be here a few more days here in the city and probably continue her master's degree here. The news was not digestible to her and she noticed some tension in every gesture Amy made with the earpiece in her ear.

That's why I didn't distract her, although I still heard some rudeness in what I was showering.

Suddenly there was a silence, I imagined that battle had ended to hold on to be with me.

I came out of the shower to rush to get dressed and start that splendid day, but I noticed a strange gesture on his face, and it wasn't because of the argument with his mother, it wasn't a regular gesture, I knew beforehand that something was going on with me.

- Who is Alice?

The first thing that came to mind was to remember that student in the literature class who insistently asked me to go out with her until one day I made the mistake of having a slip with her, obviously I couldn't answer that, I didn't even know what Alice was even talking about , but her face and the tone of voice used increased her unfortunate chances of her being that student.

- I don't know, what Alice do you mean?

I tried to do some research to see if she gave me more information, but mostly to denote astonishment and with that maybe minimize any negative consequences.

- The one who casually writes to your phone "take me again"

At that moment I could no longer say anything, I stood there paralyzed watching as she took her things and left the place, I began to cry with pain but more despair when I felt my lower limbs completely immobile, I could not advance a step and less run to stop her, it was exhausting to try, I sweated intensely and watched as it drifted almost in slow motion, I wanted to shout it also very loudly but I muted, my vocal cords no longer forced them could not emit even the slightest sound. Until I felt they were detaching inside my throat from the immense effort made to shout "Noooooo"

I woke up soaked in sweat, slowly relaxing as I smiled to see that it was a nasty nightmare. My stress gradually subsided and I prepared a relaxing cup of tea to pass that bitter drink, which was aggravated by making sure of Amy's departure, that unpleasant nightmare for moments became an intense desire for it to be reality, to see Amy when I woke up r morning with a cup of coffee prepared by her, steaming spreading the heat of her gaze. But no, he was gone, forever missing any attempt to relive the best moments of my life with a woman. In the recent dream of being true I could have amended any situation related to Alice, but in real life I had no problem to solve, I had nothing.

I felt so depressed that that negative emotion allowed me to slide my fingers on the keyboard to write the words one by one to culminate in this story, which should be ready by the end of the month for publication.

I wrote the famous "End" and sat on the couch to drink an ice-cold beer to try to erase a little the taste of her lips in my mouth.

Chapter 20

- Amy! Amy! Are you ok?

- Yes why?

- You put a face of annoyance when you were reading that book, isn't it your favorite author's?

- It was. I think I overestimated it too much.

- Are you serious? But if you told me wonders about him, isn't it that you're getting carried away by a misunderstanding?

- No, everything is well understood.

Amy was sitting on a bench in Central Park, that ideal natural space to enjoy a good book, with her friend Mafer with whom she had designed a vacation somewhere that did not remind Juan Manuel at all. However, she was tempted to read her latest work just by seeing the synopsis on the back of that book called No Destination, located in the highest and most visible part of the book store news table which they entered a day earlier to off the intense and unusual rain that fell in New York. He never thought of finding him there, and even more so among thousands of copies, having it in front of his eyes as they did when they met, seemed to be the work of chance.

Her heart palped from the moment she saw his name on that shelf, but it beat more and about to get out of her body when he read her name in the synopsis, at first instance he refused to buy it, but she had to know how that beautiful love story had culminated in fiction that beautiful love story who lived and in the end they had both separated.

The story was perfect, and even more so the surroundings of those trees with that delicious summer shade, relaxing, until it reached page 127 where they separated.

- Don't you think you're overreacting a little? You even told me that you met him when you were coming to see me, and he was going to Cincinnati.

When her friend uttered the name of that city, her mind found the relationship that existed between that city, her, him, that story and her gesture of annoyance.

She asked nothing more, only understood the reason for her anguish, waited for her to finish reading and continued to tour the tourist sites offered by the financial capital of America.

Although she did not want him to appear in places that did not relate to him, that smile appeared in every landscape, in the selfie on the statue of liberty, on her walk along Wall Street, on every screen of Time Square he saw an image of them kissing. As happened when they attended the Reds and Kiss Cam stadium surprised them and forced them to kiss the crowd gathered there.

Her attempts to make him disappear, with that reading were fruitless, though she had suspended the reading upon reaching that unpleasant part for her, curious to know what she had thought of her relationship to the end intrigued her and she finished reading that story only because of the obsession with knowing how the story inspired by them concluded.

Mafer understood this when she ordered her to sit on a park bench and without asking her to accompany her as she read the final leaves. Tears sprang from her eyes, it wasn't because of the story, that's why it lacked that story, it lacked a happy ending, a real ending, it lacked the detailed description of how to achieve happiness in an instant at the hands of a writer like him.

Chapter 21

Amy traveled very early to Mexico City, her heart was more sensitive than ever, she could almost touch the outside of what was exposed, had planned her goal millimeter, she had done nothing in months to think on that day and concentrate on that precise Moment.

Arrived at the Book Fair, JuanMa had made it a fascinating world for her to be those events where you inhale that smell of paper aged in the wood of the shelves. She sat waiting for the moment she was to execute her plan, she ordered a cup of coffee in the small cafeteria just outside the main auditorium, crowded that night. She drank too nervously to sip that elixir and enjoyed its aroma, could almost reliably remember Juanma's hands on her body in every sigh, that concoction made her feel physically along with the great emotion to which she became accustomed to being with him. While awaiting the moment he read once again in silence that poetry that he had dedicated to her in Cincinnati and that appeared in the novel "No Destiny", to grab strength and have the courage to face her destiny that day.

"Get used to it

The most beautiful years of your life are going to pass and that stupid and indescribably magical smile will probably diminish its intensity, maybe there is no longer so much joy in your gaze when mine appears, the big moments will probably disappear too ecstasy and passion, the autumn leaves of your hair may no longer fall like spring.

Time erodes everything to its devastating step, to the hardest ground, to the most precious metal, to the immense mountain.

Do you know that there are unforgettable people?

You will know now, beforehand, years before, when I tell you that we are joined by something stronger than a smile, a feeling or a passion.

You'll know when you're not with me and every step you take your mind will imagine if I agree with you, waiting for my approval to feel satisfied with yourself. Or when you're in trouble and the first thing your mind will imagine will be my lips dictating how to solve them. When you feel other lips, you will want them to be mine even when they give you great emotion, you will know that this smoothness is incomparable.

And if we ever meet again, you'll joke about how easy it's been for you to get used to me, though maybe it's in 20 years and I'd swear that that fake smile will give you away by saying inside; my body still bristles at feeling yours around.

And even if you think you can fly away, with your own wings, with your accumulated strength, you won't be able to do it apart.

It will always be present in your mind that I am the best memory of your life, with whom you congenial in everything.

So, get used to see me always even under your eyelids, it's imminent, you can't stop it, you can never, you'll never be there forever."

Those words were perfect, but, far from it, they made no sense. She knew how to wait patiently, with everything and the stress caused by the situation, like a fierce waiting to attack her prey, knowing that it is a fight that can be lethal and therefore the legs feel that tingling, they move vibrating, but they move slowly by fear , waited, until she heard the applause, the presentation was over.

It was the moment he had waited so long, to face his greatest love and hers greatest fear in a single instant, and not knowing if she could get away with it, but love always demands to risk everything, even if it is for no reason, even if it is stupidly and impulsively.

She entered that compound and went to the nearest part of the stand, her legs rumbling with the nerves of being in front of so many people and having to face it. It was minutes when she felt his frozen body and perhaps the most stressful moments of her life. The moderator asked if anyone else had any questions for the author and it was then that anger broke out there.

She raised her hand to the astonishment of the more than two hundred attendees squeezed into the main hall of the mining palace. He also felt that icy burning that was experienced when the adrenaline appeared in his life, he felt him run again at that time, but this occasion was not an adrenaline rush in the face of unwanted danger, it was the adrenaline of the thrill of having her close again and the uncertainty not knowing what words would exhale her lips, whether of novel approval, disapproval, or simply an angry claim in public for not having been what she expected in that relationship.

- Good afternoon, my name is Amy Collins and I am the most ardent admirer of Juan Manuel's work; - she made a slight pause, the nervousness did not allow her to quickly and coherently spin what she said, her hands were shaking, her voice was constantly breaking and she pressed the microphone tightly - yet "No destination" is the worst work I have ever read from the author - in unison the public exhalate loudly and notoriously in sign of surprise and some irritation, especially the organizers. - Sorry, I'm sorry to be so rude, but if you don't think my comment, - walked already safer losing fear to the front rows standing almost in front of it, like when you dip the skin in very cold water and as the seconds pass the body adapts and can enjoy the delight of floating - just as I will express it, because this story is about me, the love of his life, of which he said made him feel and vibrate every second like no one else. And acting cowardly will never be a good ending to a love novel. It would be for a coward perhaps, to retreat to avoid further losses, or sci-fi to seek an unexpected end. But if you want to talk about love Juan Manuel, - she stared at him in the eye, with that look with which she so often lived up - you can't act that way or in a novel. That story should not have ended like this, the protagonist had to fight to make Amy feel what she had never felt in her short life. For reinforcing those golden and silk castles that the best writer in the world managed to build in her life and in her mind. You can't finish a play as cowardly as you did in your real life. Your misogynistic poetry that you tell in history is nothing more than cheap talk because you do not get used to something that you do not fight for, the coward in clamor belongs nothing, only the forgetfulness and the sad comfort of the applause of an empty work as you are praising today. -

A tear flowed in that moment from her flushed cheeks. She put the microphone on the table where the author and the book's presenters were. She walked out slowly dragging the pain of disappointment on her shoulders of those who came to consider the likely love of her life, until she was lost from the sight of all the attendants who followed her stealthily with her gaze until the last fraction of a second in which the slit formed when the last millimeter of the door closed could sense his hair covering his face.

Juan Manuel was stunned, did not know what to say until someone showed up to resolve the altercation, the moderator once again urged the audience to raise their hand if anyone had any other comments.

- Let this time be a little less warlike than the past - The audience broke from the amazement of the moment before to a laugh at the moderator's comment.

There were two more participations, praising Juan Manuel's work, which indirectly attempted to erase the previous negative comment, just showing the strengths of the plot in that part where the iron criticism of that girl lay.

After the embarrassing incident everything was cordiality and the toast was a balm to relax the attendees, Juan Manuel signed all the books they brought for the event, which were sold out, perhaps because of the morbidity of the scene that had made him that protagonist of that fictional story that wasn't so fiction, or perhaps because of the author's maturity as a writer.

Now he did not attempt to make a special dedication for each, although he was satisfied by the presentation, his mind at the time had no head to create something different, his memory only remembered again and again that moment when he first kissed Amy, in which he felt that he was in paradise, had never met a woman as beautiful, charming, elegant and intelligent as her.

Amy walked many stables crying, totally heartbroken, trying to make the tiredness of walking through blocks and blocks tire her legs already weakened by the previous stress experienced and end up erasing Juan Manuel's face from her suffocated mind.

She stopped at the bookstore in front of the cathedral.

Chapter 22

She entered that bookstore on the bank of the main avenue, which Juan Manuel had told her was the vastest in the city. There he saw the prodigy son of this, the most noted writer of that small municipality of the southern state of Veracruz, in the Gulf of Mexico. His work "No Destination" was the first in the shelf of novelties, he remembered for a moment the awkward moment she felt when she met him, however, she finally accepted for herself that at that time she liked JuanMa's voice, although she resisted almost automatically as a routine and filter in front of the jerks. With that vibration of the sounds emitted from his vocal cords he felt something different from the usual, not because of her strength or originality but because of the confidence she felt when she heard each syllable on his lips.

The cover of "No Destination" was not the same as the copy put in the first place in the library of his house. No longer a lost route on the horizon, the image that adorned the work had been changed by a blurred image on a horizon facing the sun. That image immediately shook her in a split second, starting with bristling the skin on her arms and ending up on her head stunned by that unexpected blow. Yes, the image was too like the two of them on those stairs looking out at dawn the first time they made love.

She was stunned for a few minutes looking at that cover, and a few moments passed of those moments and felt in her arms, tightly held and recharged against that wall. It wasn't just excitement that I felt when I was in his arms, it was trust and protection, which I hadn't felt before.

- Miss, is something wrong? - asked the bookstore manager when he saw her motionless and staring at that book.

- No, nothing, I just wanted to know how much that book costs?

- It is $127 pesos; I recommend it is from a local author.

- Yes, I know, I'm pleased to meet him. - in saying "taste" she remembered that despite being too upset with him for not looking for her, she would still vibrate everything when she heard his name.

- Then take it, you're going to like it I'm sure.

- I have no doubt about it, do you know why they changed the cover of the book?

- Don't you know? Don't you know the writer? You don't seem to know him that well.

- Well, he doesn't call me to check out his cover changes.

- I understand, if you do not speak to ask him his cover changes neither does when he makes a new edition with a different ending.

- A different ending?

- Yes, that is due to the change of the cover, apparently the copies sold in the first edition have some differences with this.

-I don't think so, - she smiled at hearing that - what happens is that you want to sell me that copy, I imagine he gives you some commission for it. - remembered once again when he met JuanMa who told her the same thing.

- No, miss, what's more, if I'm lying to you, I'll give you your money back, the current version has some substantial changes, check it out for yourself. - put a tome on his hands.

- Ok, I'll take it, but give me a card with the store details just in case it's fake what you've told me, send the book back and wait for my refund.

- Of course, yes miss, here is my card with my name and all the contact details, you are from the north right?

- Yes, why do you mention it?

- Curiosity, her battered accent and her distrust of southerners give her away. - smiled sarcastically at Amy and handed her a bag from the store with the book inside, her note and the change of the two-hundred-peso bill she had paid with.

She took her package and headed to the corner of that block, where there was a café with several umbrellas outside where she sat down to drink an espresso while waiting for the arrival of the Uber that would take her to the airport, for moments as her thinking of changing her flight and having late with him, but it made him afraid not to get what he desired; make him feel in love again, if only for an instant.

That journey was an ordeal, it is like living the same pain of losing the love of your life twice in the same way, it was feeling that feeling that she had never felt, had never been turned away in that way and forgotten.

Every sip he gave to the café, his lips frowning with a sign of pain, of sadness, of nostalgia, of denial.

Chapter 23

She just fastened her seat belt on the plane, put a pillow behind her neck, pulled a bottle of water out of her bag and began reading which fascinated her every detail to ease a little the pain he felt when he walked away from him forever. It was like living again that September 28th at the airport in Mexico City. She even read twice the beginning to imagine hearing every word of his lips and feeling that emotion when she met him.

Until that moment each semicolon was identical to the version she had read in the first edition, she was tempted to call the book seller to claim him, when she remembered that he had mentioned that the ending was the modified one, not the beginning, just for disturbing that insistent sir and leave in wrong the most prominent writer in the country. Although for an instant she did believe that it would be the same version, when she came once more to page 127 he began the magic she had known in him, in his hands, in his lips and in his words; those that made her vibrate by reading them and dreaming when she heard them nearby.

Everything happened identical to what happened between them to the page where the previous version ended the abrupt separation of a strong and intense born relationship from its inception. There was about a quarter of history calculated by her with the thickness of the pages left to read.

That deranged anger she felt for days before seeing him in the presentation slowly morphed into a constant smile in every word she read from that book.

She ordered an espresso while she was sending it aside, that aroma of coffee had a bit of its essence and allowed her to blow her imagination in that ending that he began to like, one part intrigued him and another terrified him.

How could I have predicted I would be there?

It was unthinkable, but true. When she reached page 147 the environment was the same, so identical that he did not look like a writer with excellent imagination describing something of his mind but a seer observing how she was dressed exactly that day to enter his presentation and take the microphone.

That's how it was. Strangely in that book impossible to have been written after her visit to his presentation, it was a faithful copy of what had happened. Or he knew her so well that he could perfectly make every move predictable. She even reached the color of the dress she wore that day, and some of the accessories she was wearing.

If it was something diabolical she was terrified to think that someone could decipher that and still feel something for him, if it was a coincidence she liked to have adored his tastes because it made him think that he had it perfectly studied by the great love that had him , if it were prediction it was shocking to know that he could imagine she so well and that it could be what he thought, if it were the product of his imagination that way to connect with each other, to know it perfectly, because that only happens with those who know, loved and idolized.

She found incomprehensible her way of describing so precisely every detail of her that day she attended the presentation, the way she expected her prey to be cared for outside drinking an espresso, as if she could see the future with a magic ball and put it into a novel the one that had her excited like never before with a book.

She finished reading the ending the moment the plane landed at Culiacan airport. She kept crying with the scenes of the outcome of that story.

"Love is not only the softness of the petals of my buds gently caressing your body, they are also the bitter thorns of the lacerating words that I will tell you with my bad mood.

Not everything is honey, yet those fleeting moments we live in have not found equals in my life either. It may have been circumstantial, but it could also be just a small sample of even more intense and beautiful moments together. We'll only know that when we decide to be together."

It was a message addressed to her. Nothing would change her decision now to phone him to go and see him and try to recover what they had lived, she was no longer afraid of his rejection, she had to take high hopes, she had high hopes after reading a complete novel about how much he came to love her.

She slept like a log, calm, without the stress of not feeling loved, with the calm of having a probable future with the man who had most captivated her. Feeling the first flashes of dawn she jumped out of bed through that motivational spring called JuanMa. She took the phone and dialed several times without any answer, she found it very strange.

Arriving at work the first contact he had was with an employee of a parcel company.

- Do you know Miss Amy Collins?

- Yes, it's me.

- Sign me here, this package is for you.

When she saw that it was a package sent from Coatzacoalcos to her, she smiled, immediately went to her office and securely closed the door so no one would bother her. She opened it immediately and found an envelope with a formal invitation, like the ones they deliver to attend a wedding or fortnightly, she felt an icy sweat running through her skin thinking about the worst, maybe it was her wedding and then yes, everything was lost. She took encouragement to read the first lines and as letter progressed by letter, her skin shuddered.

"Formal invitation to watch the sunset in front of the cathedral of the city of Guasave, Sinaloa.

Time: 17:30

Location: Cathedral Cafeteria

Day: October 29, 2019

Wear casual clothing and a white blouse to recognize you"

He was laughing, always happy with the moments of his life. When he believed that she should take the initiative and take his chances, he once again did so by entering her life in an unusual but more important way, making her feel loved.

Chapter 24

She couldn't sleep all night with the great emotion she felt to see him again, it took almost an hour to choose a dress suitable for the occasion, the same happened with the slippers, the accessories, the perfume, she wanted to look perfect for such an important occasion.

She woke up very early before the rays of light appeared, the adrenaline had made her rise driven to do many things in the day, even upon seeing the hour, she realized that she could take a few turns around the house running to exercise a little. She prayed as she did every day, as a post-exercise routine and took the pills that helped her improve digestion. The routine was complete and it was only seven in the morning, it was ten hours before the appointment, which could cause her to finish with her nails because of nerves, which also reminded her to go and polish them, she also did her hair and he couldn't find what else to do to lose time to see JuanMa, that day she devoted it completely to looking spectacular. She asked permission in the office not to go, while watching the second slower swings, she died to see him, to hear the words she uttered to fall in love with her again as she did every time something came out of her lips.

Although time was too slow, the appointment time approached, and she was ready.

She carried her purse with the usual required by a lady and a copy of "No Destination" to be autographed by her favorite writer.

Arrived on point, as soon as the clock was around five pm with twenty minutes and she was walking a few feet from the cafeteria after parking on the sidewalk.

Every step her body gave froze more, her throat convulsed, her hands cooled, his chest was beating intensely, his legs wobbled barely noticeably, until she could finally reach that terrace where she could see on his back that silhouette that she could recognize miles away.

- Can I sit down?

- Of course, it's an honor for me. - got up and settled her chair back to sit down. - she couldn't take it anymore and unintentionally came out of her lips those words.

- I've missed you so much. - wanted to hug him, but the nerves made her restrain herself and wait for his reaction first.

- I more than that, I have not stopped thinking of you a single fraction of a second. - he got up from the chair and hugged her very tightly and so in his arms so many pleasant moments came to mind.

- What happened to us?

- My theory is that I was afraid to be happy with you, with the risks of living in two different worlds. What's your theory?

- I had the theory that you had lacked courage, but today you showed me that no, so there is no valid theory to prevent us from being together, is there? Where will we start now?

- Here in the cathedral of your city where one day you will get married and hope it will be with me, let's start by sitting down and ordering an espresso.

They both sat down and enjoyed the beautiful sunset of that day talking about everything that had happened, everything was calm and joy, there were no claims, it was like the day they met. It was practically the day they met again.

- How long will you be here?

- As long as it takes to know if we should never separate anymore.

- But don't stay in the hotel, it must be horrible to be alone there, apart from the tremendous expense, you better come to my house meet my mom, live with us as long as you want, and when you decide you return to your city.

- I am very sorry to do so, but I love the idea of living with your family, so if there is no inconvenience I will stay if they support me. It's my turn to pay for the visit like in football, now we'll play on your court with you as a local. And I know only one thing, that I have two options to stay here or return to Coatza, but in both options it is not contemplated to do it without you, so let us wait for this time God enlightens us to know what will be best for us.

They melted into a kiss more tender than passionate.

Chapter 25

Every day in his house living with her family was better, we were all like a big family, at times I came to imagine those same corridors of that great residence the hustle and bustle of some children glazing us even more.

I had no doubts, day by day I went planning everything to achieve my change to this city without Amy knowing.

I asked her mom's permission to use the study room to work on the new literary projects I had pending. She accepted and gave me the directions to get there, it was a very large residence, two weeks and I still did not know well where every place was located and more this place I had never visited.

I walked a few steps through that hallway full of vases and old paintings. In front of a bathroom was a room full of shelves of smelly cedar wood, full of books, the adoration of us writers, that delicious aroma forced you into that sublime room and more as you took steps further, because there were not only books, there were also countless beautiful sculptures, paintings and other attractive antiques. It gave me even more confidence to recognize the cover of "Deja Vu" in the middle of that bookcase.

There were many copies of all kinds and of all genres, from the classics of Tolstoy, Dostoyevsky, Miguel de Cervantes Saavedra, Borges, H.G. Wells, Jules Verne, Mario Benedetti, Carlos Fuentes, Juan Rulfo, Octavio Paz, Alejo Carpentier, Shakespeare, Dickens; even moderns like Dan Brown.

Before I sat down to write and sort my things, I discovered that behind the door when I locked her up there was a small library with national and international newspapers with notes of cultural events such as presentations of books by famous authors especially Spanish and English, pictorial displays in the most famous places in the world. At the last link was a small collection with newspaper articles from national media, at that time I thought that I was already invading a lot the privacy of Amy's mother who gently offered me this space to work on my novels, I was going to sit to write but then I saw that photo of me smiling, it was the time when my face looked wrinkle-free and my hair was long and abundant, I remembered the beautiful reporter who made me too nervous with her microphone while I was being born of everything, it was my first interview with the local press, I went through each answer and I was very excited to remember my beginnings in the promotion of my literature. My mind was lost reliving every moment...

"- Already to conclude, Juan Manuel, Juanelo as most of your acquaintances call you here in Coatzacoalcos, tell me and the readers of El Universal some confession that you have not made before some anecdote or experience as a writer.

I still remember her smile intimidating me, with that siege my mind was clouded, and I could only think of the classic anecdotes already told to local media. It was precisely that nerve that caused me to remember a situation like I used to make and then that image was embodied in the answer of what I used to do in my beginnings as a writer.

- There is something that I usually do when I publish my works and that I have not declared in any means, although I will tell you, Violeta, that I am sorry to confess, but as it is my first national exhibition because I think that readers of El Universal deserve to know a little more of the rascality of my person.

- That would be great, tell us

- Because as a writer what I love most is to visit bookstores and, on several occasions, I felt that overflowing and indescribable emotion of seeing some potential reader browse my stories on a news rack. I thought I could take advantage of those moments to engage in some conversation and even friendship with some of my female readers so I could perhaps meet the love of my life, if I am passionate about writing probably my perfect complement I would be an avid woman reading. That's how everyone who watched some attractive reader would approach her and offer to sign my book in exchange for buying it.

- Something like a hookup technique?

- I don't want to express it so crude, - I said, laughing, - rather a way to get close to those women who appreciate my literature.

- What else do you tell them?

- I'm sorry to say it, but, for example, usually when this happens my mind is motivated to write something of that story with that person then if you get to ask me about what I'm writing, I tell you a story about her and how I know her and so the surprise factor gives them confidence in me, even on some occasion I even had a girl accompany me walking the path from my office to where I was going.

- How low is that, and has the technique worked for you?

- So far not, most have some formal commitment which I respect a lot, but if I have cultivated very good friendships that even give me their opinions and suggestions of what I write, that

serves to feedback my works, it is an interesting strategist for obtain information of all kinds.

I still remember how I smiled nervously about confessing that misdeed of mine.

    - So, you're going to keep trying?

    - Of course, I will continue to do so.

    - What bookstore and on what date and time will you attend these days? - smiled as I questioned myself.

    - Will you catch up with me there?

I tried to intimidate her with my comment, but her response intimidated me more.

    - Why do you think I'm asking you? I will assist you to sign my book and write a story about us.

It made me tremble with nerves to think that I was serious, but fortunately she got up from the chair because the time was up and I didn't know what else to say as she said goodbye and walked away from the room where we conducted the interview."

This interview was underlined and there was more, until that review made by Eduardo Mejia of my novel "Psychoaffaire: of love and death its brief step" years ago in his column of El Universal, I could almost claim that it was practically all the interviews that had done there collected and powdered on that shelf with the collection of all my works and some data from my presentations.

That detailed analysis of my career as an author, the emphasis placed on my customs as an author and my peculiar activities led me to understand why Amy was in my life. All my memories with Amy passed through my mind dizzily confusing all my senses, not knowing how to differentiate the real from the unreal, the truth from the false, it is so complicated sometimes to understand certain things, even believe them, to be able to imagine that everything was written or that everything was planned, I was stunned to stand there. I felt deceived, manipulated and tricked.

The fire of the betrayal of deceit and manipulation hit me with all its might and devastated my foolish heart. I felt I should have guessed; it was too perfect to be real.

Chapter 26

The first time I fell in love I was deceived in the most vile way, the second I lost the love of my life by being away and not being able to defend her love at that moment, the third time I lost her for doing nothing and my inability to act. How am I going to lose her this time?

That question was in my mind millions of times. I went from loving her with all my heart and being the perfect woman to hating her and being the most ordinary and imperfect woman, I'd ever met. I've never felt so much adrenaline running through my body, I felt depressed, disappointed, deceived, angry. I wanted to have her face to face at that very moment to squeeze her shoulders and tell her that I hated her, that she hated her, that I never wanted to see her again. Thousands of tears flowed non-stop from my unembedded face.

My phase of denial at times forced me to think of many other alternatives, a real coincidence when I met her, that she would have fallen in love with those she greatly admired, that it was not part of a plan.

I started hearing the noise about the hallway of her sneakers heading to the studio, I took that letter opener from the desk, but what was I thinking? How could the idea of hurting her pass my mind? I've never been like this, but I've never felt so hurt. Every step that came up I didn't know what to do, it was like getting close to a cliff that I had to avoid getting out of there alive.

Why Amy? Why?

I felt so weak and at the same time paralyzed by the adrenaline that I couldn't move from next to the desk, I just managed to put all the memories of my interviews back in place so that she didn't know that I knew the truth, to find out if she was able to keep lying to me.

She entered the room with that big, indescribable smile that characterized her and when she saw me from the door, her face changed.

- What is going on JuanMa? - while seeing that in my hand I had the letter opener and my face was red with courage. I didn't answer and she started to worry. - JuanMa what happened, answer me, why are you crying, what happened to you? - asked as step by step slowly approached me.

My mind was still confused, so many disastrous things were going on in my head, and more when I saw her walking towards me with that way of always calming me down. I felt her soft fingers touch my cheeks trying to dry my tears, but it was impossible not to stop sprouting, she placed her hands on my cheeks to see me in the eyes, I didn't want to see her, that look would make me assuage at the time.

Cynically she took from the desk that letter I had written to her a day earlier, which later had put it there and planned to deliver it to her at night. She began to read aloud believing that was the reason for my anguish.

"Sometimes I felt like a computer, programmed to think every certain time about her, because in the least expected moments her image always appeared in my mind for no apparent reason, it might not seem so strange if she wasn't thousands of miles away and so long without seeing it. And so it appeared suddenly, in

sublime moments as when I watched the sunset over the sea and it was understandable to see her as I looked at the beauty of that work; it also appeared in sad moments as when she was far away and alone somewhere in the world, perhaps because of the melancholy of loneliness; but she also appeared in strange moments such as when I was in the middle of a presentation or when I was halfway through a sentence suddenly and forgot what I was saying. In joyful moments for some joke or some funny situation, in intense moments like when stress overloaded my thoughts, and there in that little corner of my mind where apparently there was no room for any thought between so much worry, her smile appeared.

It was beginning autumn and there I was in that city completely unknown to me, yet it was the city of the woman I adored, feeling something totally strange, inexplicable completely, of being in an unknown city so close to her and even desperate to see her and have to wait for hours that were becoming eternal.

I thought so many beautiful things before I came here but when I saw the signing on the road that said Guasave 11 km. I felt chills, I know it would seem totally silly and childish to do what I did, but well, I could not stop idealizing it, I knew that among so many people in a small town could even find it casually and if not, minimum I would have the maybe little but beautiful satisfaction for me that I'm stepping on the ground that she sometimes steps on, and that's how I came up with just walking across the country with the slogan of spending two days entering there in your city and leave the destination the choice to meet again or not. I know it sounds stupid, but it did, I didn't think of anything but just trying to tempt fate to the max and pushing it back to give me back the beautiful moments that I'm going through.

I tried to reassure the nerves of arriving and knowing if in just two days I would have any chance or not, the bet is cast, she should have already received that formal invitation, it was like flying and in 48 hours decide something so important for a heart so watching her and seeing her again, the horrible part was caused by the uncertainty of imagining the moment as those two days ran out and getting on the bus back and just taking a souvenir from the city and staying wanting to see her again sometime in a lifetime, it was like playing it all out in 48 hours, I was afraid to come back empty-handed just to see her.

I got off the bus and because I had absolutely no plan those two days, nowhere to stay, I bought a brochure of the city and thought carefully which hotel to choose to sleep those two nights, I thought for a moment until I slept one night in one hotel and another night in another , in two distant points of the city, to increase the chances of seeing her by being in two opposite places, I thought about it over and over again and finally decided to do it that way, I also decided to choose restaurants in opposite poles of the city for breakfast, lunch and dinner, I also chose to visit all the touristic and busiest places and those places like schools to increase the likelihood of seeing different types of people, seemed an exercise of probability and statistics, in case the invitation did not arise no effect on her. Dying to accidentally find her in a different place, it would be a strange but adorable experience.

But that day was already late when I arrived in the city and had had a very heavy trip and all I had to do was sleep an hour to start very early my tour of the city, which I should also do at very early hours and very late to also increase the probability to find her, it seemed an excess but among so many people it was the least I could do, I was tempted to look in the directory for her address, but I had promised to leave the destination to do the complicated part, I would just be there in the cathedral cafeteria waiting for her.

I walked through blocks and blocks around that city imagining that I walked them through her hand, with her smile by my side, passing through that cathedral where my mind imagined one day seeing her enter with a white veil excited to spend her whole life with me, I walked down every narrow street wondering if she had ever been there, if perhaps there she had had her most beautiful dreams.

I walked to sleep, but I still couldn't sleep because I just expected to see her that time and never lose her."

She made a different smile; for some reason I had dubbed her as an indescribable smile, that one was more, she was more beautiful, more dangerous, more tender, more in love, and she kept expanding more as if I were too happy while I with my left hand squeezed her tight and with my right I pointed the letter opener at her heart.

I hit her sideways on her chest. I spent a lifetime on his head before my next attempt at lethal movement.

- With you I am happy and that's all I care about.

I hugged her tightly, dropping the letter opener as she cried heartbroken as a child in her mother's arms, in every tear she let out my grudge to forget forever anything that could separate me from her. What else did it matter if this was a conspiracy, what else did it matter if she didn't love me like I do her, what else did it happen if I was a victim of her thoughts, all that mattered to me was that as long as we were together we would be immensely happy.

    - I am happy with you too JuanMa.